THE CAPTAIN'S LOST DAUGHTER

RACHEL DOWNING

CORNERSTONETALES.COM

GOODBYE BOSTON

The SS Lydia cut through the harbour waters, her sails billowing proudly against the cloudless sky. Behind her, Boston's skyline grew smaller with each passing moment. The dockside teemed with activity—handkerchiefs waving, voices calling final farewells, some faces streaked with tears while others beamed with excitement for those embarking on new adventures.

The wind carried the mingled scents of salt water, fresh tar, and the last lingering aromas of the city—baked goods and coal smoke—across the deck. Seagulls wheeled overhead, their cries piercing through the steady rhythm of waves slapping against the hull.

"Mind your step there!" A sailor called out as he hurried past with coiled rope. Children darted between barrels and crates, their laughter rising above the creak of timber and snap of canvas. Colourful pennants fluttered from the rigging, dancing in the breeze like fragments of rainbow against the vast blue expanse.

Eva pressed herself against the railing, standing on tiptoes to better see the world falling away behind them. Her golden curls whipped about her face, occasionally obscuring her view, but she pushed them back impatiently, unwilling to miss a single moment of their departure.

"Goodbye, Boston," she whispered, her bright blue eyes drinking in the receding shoreline. "Goodbye to our little house with the red door. Goodbye to the bakery where Mama used to buy sweet buns on Sundays."

Her small fingers tightened around the stitched doll clutched to her chest—a simple thing of cotton and yarn, worn soft with years of love. It had been her mother's, then hers, the stitching repaired countless times by Lydia's gentle hands before the consumption had taken her strength away.

"Mama would have loved this adventure, wouldn't she?" Eva asked the doll softly. "Crossing the ocean to England, just like in her stories."

The doll's button eyes stared back, unblinking but somehow comforting. Eva tucked it into the pocket of her dress, patting it gently before returning her attention to the horizon. The vast emptiness ahead beckoned with promise—new places, new people, perhaps even new friends. Her heart fluttered with anticipation, even as a pang of loss reminded her of all they were leaving behind.

"Will there be mermaids, do you think? Or sea monsters?" She leaned farther over the rail, scanning the waves for any sign of mysterious creatures lurking beneath the surface.

From his position near the quarterdeck, Thomas Hartwell watched his daughter's exploration with a bittersweet ache in his chest. The sea breeze ruffled his dark hair, now flecked with premature grey at the temples. His weathered face softened as Eva's delighted laugh carried across the deck.

"She has your spirit, Lydia," he murmured, his deep green eyes reflecting the ocean's changing hues. "Your curiosity. Your joy."

The memory of his wife's face rose unbidden—her bright

smile on their wedding day, her tears of happiness when Eva was born, her quiet courage during those final months. Thomas closed his eyes briefly against the sudden sting of grief.

When he opened them again, his gaze fell on Eva, so small against the vastness of sea and sky, yet somehow containing all that remained of his world. Her golden curls—so like her mother's—caught the sunlight, creating a halo around her determined little face.

Thomas' hand moved unconsciously to the brass compass hanging from his neck. The metal was warm against his skin, a familiar weight that had guided him through countless voyages. His father had given it to him when he first went to sea, just as his grandfather had done before that.

"We're sailing a new course now, old friend," he said, running his thumb over the worn engraving on its surface. The compass had always pointed him home; now it would lead them to a new beginning.

He steadied himself against the gentle roll of the deck, watching as Eva pointed excitedly at something in the distance—perhaps a diving seabird or leaping fish. Despite everything, despite the hollow ache that had become his constant companion since Lydia's passing, Thomas felt a flicker of hope.

Liverpool awaited them across the vast Atlantic. A new position, new prospects, and perhaps, God willing, healing for them both.

A NEW THRILL

*E*va woke to the gentle rocking of the ship, sunlight streaming through the small porthole of the cabin she shared with her father. The second day at sea dawned bright and clear, with nothing but endless blue stretching in every direction. After breakfast, while her father consulted with the first mate about their course, Eva ventured out to explore.

She clutched her doll tightly as she navigated the narrow passages, nodding politely to sailors who tipped their caps at the captain's daughter. The wooden boards creaked beneath her feet, and the scent of salt and tar filled her nostrils as she emerged onto the deck.

The wind whipped her curls about her face as she made her way toward the foredeck, drawn by the magnificent view of the bowsprit cutting through waves. As she approached, she noticed a boy standing alone at the railing, his light brown hair ruffled by the breeze. He seemed lost in thought, gazing out at the horizon with an intensity that made Eva pause.

He turned at the sound of her footsteps, and their eyes met. For a moment, neither spoke. Then his face broke into a hesitant smile that Eva returned, feeling suddenly shy.

"Hello," she ventured, stepping closer.

"Hello," he replied, straightening his posture slightly. He was taller than her by several inches, perhaps twelve years old to her eight. His hazel eyes sparkled with intelligence and something else—loneliness, perhaps.

His gaze dropped to the doll clutched in her hands. "That's a beautiful doll," he said, the observation breaking the awkward silence between them.

Eva held it out for his inspection. "She was my mother's. Her name is Lydia, like Mama."

"The ship is called Lydia too," the boy pointed out.

"Papa named it after her when he was still a naval officer," Eva explained, pride warming her voice. "He says it's so she can still travel with us, even though she's gone to heaven."

The boy nodded solemnly. "I'm William Ansley," he offered, extending his hand as he'd seen adults do.

Eva shifted her doll to her left arm and shook his hand with surprising formality. "Evangeline Hartwell. But everyone calls me Eva."

"Are you travelling to England with your father, then?"

"Yes! Papa's got a new position managing a shipping company in Liverpool." Her blue eyes brightened with excitement. "Have you been to England before? What's it like?"

William laughed, a warm sound that made his whole face light up. "I live there—in London. My father's a merchant. We've been in Boston for his business."

"Oh!" Eva bounced on her toes. "Then you must know all about England! Is it truly as wonderful as in the storybooks?"

Something in her spirited curiosity seemed to break through William's reserve. He leaned against the railing, suddenly eager to share. "Parts of it are. London has grand buildings and parks and the Thames River running through it. But it rains quite a lot."

"I don't mind rain," Eva declared. "It makes everything smell fresh and clean."

William studied her with newfound interest. Most children he knew complained endlessly about being kept indoors during rainy days.

"Would you like to sit?" he asked, gesturing to a sheltered spot near the bow where crates created a natural alcove away from the bustle of the sailors.

Eva nodded eagerly, and they settled into their makeshift hideaway. The ship sailed smoothly across calm seas, the rhythmic creaking of timber creating a peaceful backdrop for their conversation.

"Tell me about Boston," William requested. "I didn't see much beyond the hotel and my father's meetings."

Eva's face lit up. "Oh, it's wonderful! There's a market where fishermen bring their catch every morning—all silvery and flapping. And bakeries with windows full of bread and pastries." Her expression softened. "Before Mama got sick, we'd have picnics by the harbour. She'd pack sweet buns and tell me stories about mermaids while Papa was at sea."

William listened, enraptured by her descriptions of cobblestone streets and church bells, secret gardens and bustling wharves.

"What about London?" Eva asked when she'd exhausted her stories. "Is it very grand?"

"Parts are," William nodded. "There's Buckingham Palace where the Queen lives, and Westminster Abbey that took hundreds of years to build." His eyes gleamed with excitement. "But I like the docks best. Ships come from everywhere—India, China, Africa—bringing spices and silks and strange animals."

"Have you seen elephants?" Eva gasped.

"Once! At a travelling exhibition." William grew animated, gesturing with his hands. "Father's business takes him everywhere. He's been to the Caribbean and seen flying fish leap from the water. And to Egypt where there are pyramids taller than church steeples."

"Will you travel too, when you're grown?"

"Absolutely," William declared. "I'll visit every country and sail every sea."

"Perhaps I'll be a great explorer too," Eva decided, her expression determined.

As the afternoon sun warmed the deck, they abandoned their quiet conversation for more active pursuits. William taught Eva how to play shuffleboard using makeshift discs fashioned from barrel lids. They raced from stern to bow, dodging between laughing sailors who good-naturedly stepped aside for the children.

"Pretend we're explorers," Eva suggested as dusk approached, painting the sky in brilliant oranges and pinks. "Searching for undiscovered lands!"

William grabbed a discarded piece of parchment from near the navigator's cabin. With a stub of charcoal, they drew an elaborate map, complete with sea monsters in the corners and mysterious islands marked with X's.

"This is Mermaid Cove," Eva insisted, pointing to a jagged coastline William had drawn.

"And here," William added, sketching mountains, "dragons sleep in caves filled with treasure."

Their laughter carried across the deck as they plotted imaginary journeys, the ship's gentle motion beneath them a promise of real adventures to come. In William's company, Eva felt the sting of leaving Boston fade, replaced by the thrill of new friendship and the boundless possibilities that lay ahead across the vast Atlantic.

A JOURNEY TO HEALING

*A*s twilight descended upon the SS Lydia, Eva and William claimed their spot near the bow. Each evening since their first meeting, they'd established this ritual—watching as the fiery sun melted into the endless horizon, painting the sky in magnificent streaks of amber and violet.

Eva hugged her knees to her chest, her doll nestled safely beside her. "Do you think the stars are the same in England as they are in Boston?"

William tilted his head back, studying the first pinpricks of light emerging in the darkening canvas above. "The same stars, just seen from a different place. My tutor taught me about constellations—like that one." He pointed upward. "That's Ursa Major, the Great Bear."

"Papa showed me that one too!" Eva's eyes widened with delight. "Mama used to say stars are windows where angels peek through to watch over us."

A comfortable silence settled between them as more stars appeared, brilliant against the deepening blue. The gentle rhythm of waves against the hull provided a soothing backdrop to their thoughts.

"Do you miss her terribly?" William asked softly. "Your mother?"

Eva nodded, her golden curls catching the last remnants of daylight. "Some days I can hardly remember what she looked like. Then I'll catch a scent—lavender or fresh bread—and suddenly she's there again." Her small fingers traced patterns on the wooden deck. "I kept one of her handkerchiefs. It still smells like her, but Papa says eventually that will fade too."

William reached over and squeezed her hand briefly. "My mother's always busy with London society. Sometimes weeks pass where I hardly see her except at formal dinners."

"That sounds lonely," Eva whispered.

"It is." William's voice carried a resignation unusual for his twelve years. "But I have grand plans. When I'm older, I'll travel everywhere—to the silk markets of China, the spice islands of Indonesia, even the frozen lands up north."

"I wish I could see all those places too," Eva sighed. "But mostly, I'd like to be a teacher someday. In Boston, I used to help the younger children on our street learn their letters."

"You'd make a splendid teacher," William declared with such certainty that Eva beamed.

"What are you two conspirators plotting now?" Thomas Hartwell's deep voice carried across the deck as he approached, his tall figure silhouetted against the ship's lanterns.

"Papa!" Eva patted the space beside her. "We're watching stars appear. Come sit with us!"

Her father settled his frame next to his daughter, nodding respectfully to William. "Master Ansley."

"Captain Hartwell," William replied with the formal politeness his upbringing demanded.

Eva leaned against her father's shoulder. "William knows all about constellations, just like you taught me."

Her father gazed upward, his weathered face softening in the fading light. The brass compass hung from his neck, catching occasional glints from the lanterns. For a moment, watching Eva's animated conversation with her new friend, the constant ache in his chest eased slightly.

"Did I ever tell you about the time I navigated purely by stars?" Thomas asked, his voice warming with the memory. "We were caught in a terrible storm off the coast of Portugal. Lightning struck our ship and damaged our navigation instruments."

Both children leaned forward eagerly.

"The clouds parted just enough after midnight that I could make out Polaris—the North Star." Her father pointed skyward. "With nothing but that star and my sextant, we charted a course to the nearest port through treacherous waters."

"Were you frightened, sir?" William asked, eyes wide.

"A good sailor respects the sea's power but doesn't surrender to fear," her father replied. "Much like life itself—we acknowledge its challenges but continue forward nonetheless."

Eva gazed at her father with undisguised admiration. In these rare moments when he shared stories from his naval days, she glimpsed the man he'd been before grief had etched deep lines around his eyes.

"Will you teach me to navigate by stars, Papa?" she asked.

Her father smiled, a genuine smile that reached his eyes. "Of course, my little one. It's a skill worth having." His large hand gently smoothed her windblown curls. "Your mother always said you had a natural sense of direction—even as a tiny child."

The mention of Lydia didn't bring the usual shadow across his features. Instead, surrounded by the vastness of the ocean and the innocent wonder of the children, Thomas seemed momentarily unburdened.

"Look!" William pointed excitedly as a streak of light cut across the sky. "A falling star!"

"Make a wish," Eva whispered, closing her eyes tightly.

Thomas watched his daughter's face, illuminated by

starlight, and made his own silent wish—that somehow, this journey would lead them both toward healing.

CALM BEFORE THE STORM

    *E*va awoke to a peculiar stillness. For days, the gentle rocking of the SS Lydia had become as natural as breathing, but this morning something felt different. The familiar creaking of timber had taken on a deeper, more ominous tone, and the light filtering through the small cabin window seemed oddly muted.

She dressed quickly, tucking her mother's doll safely into her belt before making her way to the deck. The moment she stepped outside, Eva understood the change. The brilliant blue skies that had blessed their journey had vanished, replaced by a canvas of charcoal clouds stretching to the horizon. The air felt heavy, electric with anticipation.

Sailors moved with urgent purpose, their usual banter replaced by clipped commands. They secured cargo, doubled ropes, and battened down hatches with grim efficiency. One man climbed the rigging like a spider, his movements swift as he adjusted the sails that now strained against the freshening wind.

"Eva." Her father's voice startled her. Her father stood tall, his naval bearing more pronounced than she'd seen since leaving

THE CAPTAIN'S LOST DAUGHTER

Boston. His eyes constantly scanned the darkening horizon, his hand resting on the brass compass at his chest. "You should return below deck, little one."

"Is it a storm, Papa?" she asked, though she already knew the answer.

He knelt before her, placing his hands on her shoulders. "Yes. A significant one, I fear." His voice remained steady, but Eva noticed the tightness around his eyes. "The first mate believes we'll encounter rough seas by nightfall."

Eva's stomach tightened with apprehension. She'd heard stories of storms at sea—terrible tales of ships swallowed by waves tall as church steeples. Yet looking at her father's resolute expression, she found herself caught between fear and a strange trust in his capability.

"Are you frightened?" she whispered.

A flicker of something—vulnerability, perhaps—crossed his features before disappearing behind the mask of certainty he wore for her benefit. "I respect the sea's power, Eva. As should you. But this ship is sturdy, and her crew experienced."

Eva nodded, trying to mirror his composure though her heart fluttered like a trapped bird. "I'll be brave, Papa."

His eyes softened. "You always are, my little one. So much like your mother." He pressed a kiss to her forehead before rising. "Now, find young Master Ansley and enjoy what remains of the calm. I must assist the crew."

As her father strode away, Eva felt the weight of his concern despite his reassurances. She searched the deck until she spotted William near the bow, his face turned toward the approaching darkness.

"They say it's going to be quite a blow," William said as she approached, attempting nonchalance though his voice wavered slightly. "The quartermaster told me we might see waves twenty feet high."

Eva's eyes widened. "Will the ship hold?"

William nodded with forced confidence. "Of course. English ships are built for the Atlantic's tempers."

They stood side by side, watching the increasing choppy waters. Despite the looming danger, Eva found comfort in William's presence—this unexpected friendship had brightened her journey.

"When we reach England," William said suddenly, "you must visit London. I could show you the Tower and Westminster Abbey. There's a magnificent bookshop near my father's offices that you'd adore."

Eva smiled, grateful for this glimpse of a future beyond the gathering storm. "I'd like that very much."

A massive crack of thunder rolled across the sky, making them both jump. The first fat raindrops began to fall, splattering the deck.

"Promise?" Eva asked, extending her small hand.

William took it, his grip firm despite the fear evident in his eyes. "Promise."

The ship lurched beneath them as the first large wave struck its bow, sending spray across the deck. Their hands separated as they grabbed for support, exchanging one final look of determination before the world around them began to tilt and heave.

CRASHING WAVES

𝒯he rain began to fall in earnest now, heavy droplets striking the deck with increasing force. Eva gripped the railing as the SS Lydia pitched forward, then back, the gentle roll of previous days transformed into something violent and unpredictable. William stumbled toward her, his face pale against the darkening sky.

"We should go below," he shouted over the rising wind, but Eva couldn't move. Her eyes were fixed on the horizon where monstrous clouds, black as coal dust, churned and boiled like a witch's cauldron. The sea beneath had turned from blue to an angry slate grey, white-capped waves growing taller with each passing minute.

A flash of lightning split the sky, illuminating the deck in stark relief. In that instant, Eva saw the fear etched on every sailor's face—men who had spent their lives at sea now moved with urgent, jerky motions, their usual confidence replaced by grim determination.

"Eva!" Her father's voice cut through the chaos. He strode across the deck, somehow maintaining his balance despite the ship's increasingly erratic movements. "Get below now, both of you!"

But before they could move, a massive wave crashed against the starboard side. The ship lurched violently, sending Eva sprawling. She felt the rough planks scrape her palms as she tried to catch herself. Water cascaded over the rails, soaking her dress and plastering her golden curls against her face.

"I've got you." Her father's strong hands lifted her to her feet. All around them, sailors scrambled to secure loose cargo while others climbed the rigging, fighting to reef the sails that strained against the gale.

Thomas' voice carried across the deck, clear and commanding. "Secure that main line! Johnson, get those barrels below deck! Richards, help with the foresail before it tears!"

The men responded instantly to his orders, his naval experience evident in every confident command. Eva watched, mesmerised by this transformation in her father—no longer the quiet, grief-stricken man of recent months, but a leader whose very presence inspired confidence.

A particularly violent pitch sent Eva stumbling against her father's legs. She clutched at his coat, feeling the rough wool beneath her fingers. The ship creaked ominously, timbers groaning under the assault of wind and wave.

"Papa, I'm frightened," she whispered, reaching into her pocket for her mother's doll. The small, worn figure offered little comfort against the howling tempest, but she clutched it tightly nonetheless.

Her father knelt beside her, his hands gripping her shoulders firmly. Rain streamed down his face, dripping from his chin as he looked intently into her eyes.

"Listen to me, Eva. This storm is fierce, but you are fiercer." His voice was steady, a lifeline in the chaos. "Remember what I told you about the stars? Even when clouds hide them, they're still there, guiding us home."

THE CAPTAIN'S LOST DAUGHTER

Eva nodded, swallowing her fear. "Like Mama watches over us even though we can't see her."

Something flickered in her father's eyes—pride, perhaps, or pain. "Exactly like that, my brave girl."

Another wave crashed over the bow, drenching them both. Thomas pulled Eva closer, shielding her with his body as he scanned the deck. William had found shelter near the companionway, clutching a rope with white-knuckled hands.

"Stay close to me," Her father ordered, his voice cutting through the wind's howl. "Both of you. We need to—"

His words were cut short by a deafening crack. The mainmast swayed dangerously as a portion of rigging snapped, whipping through the air like a giant serpent. Sailors scattered, shouting warnings as the heavy ropes lashed the deck.

"All hands! Secure that line!" Her father roared, pushing Eva toward William. "Stay with him. Don't move until I return."

Eva watched in horror as her father charged toward the danger, joining several sailors who struggled to control the thrashing ropes. The ship pitched violently, nearly vertical as it climbed a massive wave, then plunged down the other side. Eva fell hard against the deck, the breath knocked from her lungs.

William grabbed her arm, helping her to a more sheltered position near the bulkhead. "Hold on!" he shouted, his face a mask of terror that surely mirrored her own.

Through the sheets of rain, Eva watched the crew's desperate battle against the elements. Her father moved with purpose, directing men with confident gestures even as water poured over the rails. The brass compass gleamed at his throat whenever lightning flashed, a small beacon in the darkness.

Suddenly, the ship gave a tremendous lurch. Eva heard splintering wood and men's shouts turning to screams. A massive wave, taller than the mainmast itself, loomed over the starboard side.

"The boats! Lower the boats!" someone screamed.

Chaos erupted as passengers emerged from below, their faces contorted with panic. Sailors rushed to the lifeboats, struggling to lower them into the churning sea. Eva felt herself being pulled along in the crush of bodies, separated from William by the surging crowd.

"Papa!" she screamed, searching desperately for her father's familiar figure. "PAPA!"

Through a break in the crowd, she spotted him helping a woman with a small child toward one of the boats. Their eyes met across the deck, and he fought his way toward her, battling both the storm and the panicked passengers.

"Eva!" He reached her at last, lifting her into his arms. "Hold tight to me."

He carried her to the nearest lifeboat, where sailors struggled to maintain order as passengers clamoured to board. He placed Eva gently into the small craft, his hands lingering on her shoulders.

"Get in, Papa," she pleaded, clutching at his sodden coat. "Please!"

Her father pressed a kiss to her forehead, his lips warm despite the freezing rain. "I'll be right behind you, my angel. I need to help the others first."

"No!" Eva reached for him desperately as the boat began to lower. "Don't leave me!"

"I'll never leave you," he promised, his green eyes intense with determination. "Be brave for me."

Before Eva could protest further, a tremendous wave crashed against the ship's side. The deck tilted sharply, sending passengers sliding across the wet planks. Thomas turned instinctively, lunging to catch a young woman who was about to be swept overboard.

"PAPA!" Eva screamed as the lifeboat descended toward the raging sea, her father's figure growing smaller against the dark hulk of the dying ship.

The last she saw of him was his face turned toward her, one hand raised in farewell or reassurance, before another wave crashed over the deck, obscuring him from view.

OVERBOARD

The lifeboat plunged toward the churning sea, suspended by ropes that seemed too frail for such precious cargo. Eva clutched the wooden seat, her knuckles white, eyes fixed on the ship where her father still stood. Rain lashed her face, mingling with hot tears as the distance between them grew.

A tremendous wave lifted the small craft, then dropped it with sickening speed. Eva's stomach lurched as they hit the water with a crash that rattled her bones. The sailors struggled with the oars, fighting to push away from the doomed ship's massive hull.

"Row! For Heaven's sake, row!" a man shouted, his voice barely audible above the storm's fury.

Eva kept her gaze locked on the SS Lydia, searching desperately for her father's figure among the chaos of the tilting deck. Lightning split the sky, illuminating the ship in stark relief—a wounded beast making its final stand against the merciless sea.

Then came the sound. A thunderous roar that seemed to rise from the ocean's depths, followed by the tortured groan of

THE CAPTAIN'S LOST DAUGHTER

splintering wood and twisting metal. The Lydia tilted sharply, its bow rising as the stern began to sink.

"Papa!" Eva screamed, half-rising from her seat until a woman pulled her back down.

Through sheets of rain, Eva watched in horror as passengers slid across the deck toward the churning water. Her father appeared at the railing, helping a young boy—was it William?—before turning to reach for others slipping past him. His powerful arms stretched out, grabbing for hands that disappeared one by one into the darkness.

The ship tilted further, nearly vertical now. Thomas clung to a rope, still trying to pull someone to safety when the rope snapped. Eva saw him scramble for purchase on the slick deck, his body sliding inexorably toward the waiting sea.

"NO!" The scream tore from her throat, raw and primal.

The Lydia gave one final, shuddering groan before plunging beneath the waves. In a heartbeat, the water engulfed the deck where her father had stood. The massive ship vanished with terrifying speed, leaving nothing but churning foam and scattered debris where it had been.

"Papa! PAPA!" Eva's cries were lost in the howling wind, her small body shaking with the force of her grief. "Please, no! Please!"

The lifeboat rocked violently, nearly capsizing as waves crashed over its sides. Around her, strangers clung to each other and the boat's edges, their faces masks of terror in the lightning flashes. A woman wept quietly beside Eva, clutching a sodden shawl to her chest. A bearded man bailed frantically with his hat, his movements desperate and mechanical.

Eva's world had contracted to a single thought: her father was gone. Swallowed by the same cruel sea that had taken their ship. The compass that never left his neck, the strong hands that had lifted her high above his head, the voice that had told her stories of far-off places—all gone in an instant.

"The stars," she whispered, her voice breaking as she raised her tear-streaked face to the storm-black sky. "You said they'd guide us home."

But there were no stars tonight, no gentle light to show the way. Only darkness and the relentless pounding of the waves against their fragile craft.

Hours passed, or perhaps only minutes—time had lost all meaning. The lifeboat rose and fell with sickening regularity, water sloshing around their ankles despite the constant bailing. Eva sat numb and silent, her mother's doll clutched to her chest, the only family she had left in the world.

The storm's fury began to abate as dawn approached, the waves gradually subsiding from mountains to hills. In the grey half-light, Eva could see other lifeboats scattered across the water, tiny islands of humanity in the vast emptiness. Of the Lydia, there was no sign—not even floating wreckage remained to mark its passing.

"Land!" The cry came from a sailor at the bow, his arm extended toward the horizon. "I can see land!"

Heads turned, hope flickering across exhausted faces. Eva looked too, squinting at the dark smudge that might be salvation. Would her father somehow be there, waiting? The thought bloomed in her heart despite everything she had seen.

"We're saved!" someone shouted. "Thank God, we're saved!"

The lifeboat surged forward on a sudden swell, riding high for one glorious moment. Eva glimpsed the distant shore, tantalisingly close—then felt the world tilt as the craft caught in a crosscurrent.

"Hold fast!" the sailor shouted, but his warning came too late.

The lifeboat flipped with shocking speed. Eva felt herself airborne for one breathless moment before the cold water closed over her head. The shock drove the air from her lungs as she tumbled through the darkness, unable to tell up from down.

Her last conscious thought was of her father's face, smiling as he pointed to the stars. Then all went black.

WASHED ASHORE

The first rays of morning sunlight pierced through dissipating storm clouds, casting an ethereal glow across the wreckage-strewn beach. Fragments of wood, torn fabric, and unidentifiable debris littered the dark sand like forgotten memories of the previous night's violence.

Among this chaos, a small figure lay motionless where the tide had deposited her. As a wave retreated back to sea, Eva's body convulsed suddenly. Water erupted from her mouth as she coughed violently, her lungs fighting to expel the ocean that had nearly claimed her. She rolled onto her side, retching and gasping, each breath a painful victory.

Consciousness returned in painful fragments. The coarse sand against her cheek. The salt burning her throat. The hollow ache where her heart should be.

"Papa," she whispered, the word barely audible over the gentle lapping of waves that now seemed mockingly peaceful.

Eva pushed herself up on trembling arms, her soaked dress heavy against her small frame. Her curls hung in tangled, salt-stiffened ropes around her face as she surveyed her surroundings with disbelieving eyes. Dark sand stretched in both directions, bordered by jagged rocks that rose like accusing fingers toward the brightening sky. In the distance, smoke rose from chimneys in what appeared to be a small village nestled against the hillside.

A sudden panic seized her as she patted the sand around her. "No, no, no," she muttered frantically until her fingers closed around a sodden bundle. Her mother's doll—somehow still clutched in her grasp or caught in her clothing during her tumble through the water. The stitched face stared back at her, one button eye missing, the fabric darkened by seawater.

Eva pressed the doll to her chest and released a sob that seemed to come from the very depths of her being. The sound echoed across the empty beach, unanswered.

"The boat," she murmured, scanning the horizon. But there was no sign of the lifeboat or its occupants. No indication of other survivors. Just endless water meeting endless sky, with no hint of the tragedy that had unfolded hours before.

Using a piece of driftwood for support, Eva struggled to her feet. Her legs trembled beneath her, threatening to collapse with each step as she oriented herself toward the distant village. Smoke meant fire. Fire meant people. People might mean help.

The journey across the beach seemed endless. Twice she fell to her knees, and twice she forced herself up again, clutching her doll and whispering words of encouragement as if speaking to a younger child. "We must keep going. We must find help. Papa would want us to be brave."

As she approached the outskirts of the village, the sound of human voices reached her ears—normal, everyday conversations that felt surreal after the night of terror she had endured. A woman laughed somewhere nearby, the sound cutting through Eva's fog of despair like a knife.

The village consisted of simple stone cottages with thatched roofs, fishing nets hung to dry between poles, and small boats pulled up on the shore beyond the main beach. Life continued here, untouched by the disaster that had torn her world apart.

Near one of the boats, a woman worked alone, her weathered hands moving deftly as she repaired a fishing net. She hummed softly to herself, her round face peaceful in concentration. Grey-streaked brown hair was tucked beneath a simple kerchief, and her sturdy frame spoke of a lifetime of physical work.

Eva stumbled closer, her strength finally giving way as she collapsed onto the sand. The sound alerted the woman, who looked up sharply, her warm brown eyes widening at the sight of the bedraggled child.

"Good Heavens!" The woman dropped her netting and hurried over, concern etched across her features. She knelt beside Eva, gentle hands assessing for injuries. "Child, where have you come from?"

Eva opened her mouth to respond, but only a broken sob emerged. The woman's kind face blurred through her tears.

"There now, love. You're safe." The woman slipped off her woollen shawl and wrapped it around Eva's trembling shoulders. The sudden warmth made Eva realise how cold she'd been, her body shaking uncontrollably now.

"I'm Mrs Fisher—Gemma Fisher. And you, poor thing, look like you've been through the very devil himself." Her accent was different from the Boston voices Eva knew, but the kindness in her tone transcended any such differences.

Eva clutched the edges of the shawl, drawing it tighter around herself. "Our ship," she managed finally, her voice raw from salt and screaming. "The Lydia. It sank in the storm."

Mrs Fisher's expression softened with understanding and sorrow. "Oh, child. Were you alone?"

"My father—" Eva's voice broke. She clutched her doll tighter. "He was helping others when the ship went down. I was in a lifeboat, but it overturned near the shore."

Mrs Fisher gently brushed wet hair from Eva's forehead. "What's your name, love?"

"Evangeline Hartwell. Eva." The simple act of stating her name brought fresh tears. Who was she now, without her father? Without William? Without anyone?

"Well, Eva Hartwell, you've shown remarkable courage making it this far." Mrs Fisher's voice was steady, grounding. "I lost my husband to the sea three years past. The ocean gives life to our village, but it takes as well. That's the way of things here." Mrs Fisher eyes filled with a bittersweet melancholy. "God must have a plan for you."

She helped Eva to her feet, supporting her with a strong arm. "Come along to my cottage. We'll get you dry and warm, with something hot in your belly. Then we can sort what's to be done."

As they walked slowly toward the village, Mrs Fisher continued speaking, her voice a soothing balm. "Our little community has weathered many storms, both the kind that rage at sea and the kind that rage in our hearts. We look after our own here. And for now, at least, you're one of us."

For the first time since the storm began, Eva felt a tiny flicker of something other than despair. Not hope, exactly—it was too soon for that—but perhaps its distant cousin: the possibility that she might survive this, somehow.

The cottage door opened before them, spilling warm light onto the path. Eva stepped over the threshold, still clutching her doll, still wrapped in Mrs Fisher's shawl, still broken—but no longer alone.

MRS FISHER'S COTTAGE

Mrs Fisher's cottage was small but immaculately kept. Eva stood just inside the doorway, dripping seawater onto the worn wooden floor as her eyes adjusted to the warm glow of the hearth fire. The single room served as kitchen, dining area and living space all at once, with a narrow staircase leading to what Eva presumed was a sleeping loft above.

"Let's get you out of those wet things first," Mrs Fisher said, guiding Eva toward the fire. "I have some old clothes that might do until yours dry."

Eva nodded mutely, still clutching her mother's doll. The familiar scents of freshly baked bread and simmering stew filled the air, reminding her painfully of home—of her father's rare days off when they would cook together, of her mother's recipes that her father had carefully preserved after her death.

Mrs Fisher disappeared briefly up the narrow stairs, returning with a simple cotton nightdress and woollen shawl. "These belonged to my daughter," she explained, her voice softening. "She's grown and married now, lives two villages over."

With gentle efficiency, Mrs Fisher helped Eva change behind

a small privacy screen, exclaiming softly at the bruises that marked the child's arms and legs from her ordeal. Once dressed in the dry clothes, Eva felt the first hint of warmth returning to her bones.

"There now," Mrs Fisher said, settling Eva at the small wooden table. "Let's put something in that empty stomach."

The walls around them were adorned with simple treasures —a large fish preserved and mounted on a wooden plaque, fishing nets draped decoratively in corners, and a collection of sea glass arranged on the windowsill. A portrait of a robust man with kind eyes hung above the mantle—Mrs Fisher's husband, Eva guessed, now claimed by the same sea that had taken her father.

Mrs Fisher placed a bowl of steaming fish stew before Eva, along with a thick slice of brown bread still warm from baking. "Eat slowly now," she cautioned. "Your stomach needs gentle treatment after such a trial."

Eva hadn't realised how hungry she was until the first spoonful touched her lips. The rich, salty broth and tender chunks of white fish tasted like life itself. She forced herself to eat slowly as instructed, savouring each bite as though it might be her last.

"Do they know?" Eva asked suddenly, her voice small. "About the ship? Will they be looking for survivors?"

Mrs Fisher paused in her own eating, considering her words carefully. "Word travels quickly along the coast when there's a wreck. The authorities will be searching, yes. And when you're stronger, we'll go into the larger town to report you safe."

Eva nodded, hope flickering in her chest for the first time. "Then they might find my father too. He's an excellent swimmer. Captain Thomas Hartwell—he was in the Royal Navy before." The words tumbled out, as though speaking them might make them truer. "He always said a good sailor never gives up."

Mrs Fisher's eyes softened with something Eva recognised as

pity, but she didn't contradict the child's hope. "Finish your stew, love. Tomorrow is soon enough to think about what comes next."

That night, wrapped in clean blankets on a small trundle bed Mrs Fisher had prepared near the fire, Eva allowed herself to imagine her father walking up the path to the cottage door, his familiar stride and warm smile intact. In this dream-like state between waking and sleeping, she could almost believe it might happen.

JOY & GRIEF

*D*ays melted into one another as Eva adjusted to life in the fishing village. Mrs Fisher had introduced her to the small community, where she was met with kind words and sympathetic glances. The village folk knew the sea's cruelty intimately—every family had lost someone to its depths at some point.

"Like this," Mrs Fisher demonstrated, her weathered hands moving deftly as she repaired a fishing net. "See how the knot must be tight but not so tight it pulls the whole net askew?"

Eva mimicked the movement, her smaller fingers growing more confident with each attempt. "My father taught me to tie sailor's knots," she said, the memory bringing both pain and comfort. "He said I had clever hands."

"And so you do," Mrs Fisher agreed, watching Eva complete the repair perfectly. "You're a quick study, Eva Hartwell."

The days developed a rhythm—mornings spent helping with chores, afternoons often dedicated to mending nets or baking bread, evenings passed in quiet conversation by the fire. Mrs Fisher never pressed Eva to speak of the shipwreck, but she listened attentively when memories surfaced naturally.

"I had a friend on the ship," Eva said one evening as they sat shelling peas. "William Ansley. He was twelve and knew all about the stars. He was going to show me London someday."

Mrs Fisher nodded, her hands never stopping their work. "Perhaps he still will."

In these moments, Eva felt almost normal—almost as though she belonged in this small cottage with its sea-worn treasures and comforting smells. But nights remained difficult territory.

The first time she woke screaming, Mrs Fisher was at her side in moments, stroking her hair and murmuring soothing words until the terror subsided.

"I saw him again," Eva whispered, tears streaming down her face. "Papa was reaching for me, but the water kept pulling him away."

"Dreams have power, little one," Mrs Fisher said, her voice steady in the darkness. "But they cannot hurt you here."

The nightmares continued—visions of roiling black water, splintering wood, and her father's face disappearing beneath the waves. Some nights Eva would wake to find herself already wrapped in Mrs Fisher's arms, the woman having heard her whimpers before they escalated to screams.

"Will they ever stop?" Eva asked one morning, exhausted from another night of fragmented sleep.

Mrs Fisher was kneading bread dough, her strong arms working rhythmically. "In time," she said thoughtfully. "Grief is like the tide, Eva. It comes in waves, overwhelming at first. But gradually, the waves grow farther apart, less powerful. They never stop completely—I still dream of my Bertram sometimes—but they become manageable."

She paused her kneading to look directly at Eva. "The heart heals at its own pace. There's no rushing it, no forcing it. All we can do is keep living, one day at a time, and honour those we've lost by finding joy where we can. Time and God's grace heals all wounds."

That evening, as they sat by the fire with Mrs Fisher teaching her to knit, Eva felt a curious sensation in her chest—a warmth that wasn't quite happiness but wasn't entirely sorrow either. Mrs Fisher was telling a funny story about her husband's first disastrous attempt at baking bread, and Eva found herself laughing despite everything.

The sound of her own laughter startled her, bringing an immediate wave of guilt. How could she laugh when her father might still be fighting for his life somewhere? When William might be lost forever?

Mrs Fisher seemed to read her thoughts. "Joy doesn't dishonour grief, child," she said gently. "They live side by side in us, like the sun and moon in the sky. Both are necessary."

Eva nodded, not entirely convinced but willing to consider it. As she picked up her knitting again, the rhythmic click of needles soothed her frayed nerves. Outside, the eternal sound of waves against the shore continued—a reminder of what she had lost, but also, somehow, a promise that life continued regardless.

WINTER'S CHILL

A month passed, then two. The warm days of autumn gradually surrendered to winter's advance. Eva noticed the change in more than just weather—faces in the village grew tighter, conversations more hushed. When she and Mrs Fisher visited the market, fewer fish lay in the stalls, and prices had climbed higher.

"Not much of a catch today," muttered Old Tom, the fishmonger who usually greeted them with a cheerful wink. Today his eyes skittered past Eva to Mrs Fisher. "Hard times coming, Gemma. Hard times indeed."

Eva pretended to examine a small mackerel while straining to hear their conversation.

"We'll manage," Mrs Fisher replied, though her voice lacked its usual confidence. "We always do."

"Aye, but it's different now, isn't it?" Tom's gaze flicked meaningfully toward Eva. "Another mouth changes things."

That night, Eva lay awake listening to the wind rattling the cottage windows. Mrs Fisher had been quieter than usual during supper, measuring portions carefully and eating less than her share. Eva wasn't a fool—she'd seen the nearly empty flour barrel, the dwindling stack of firewood.

The next morning, she rose early and attacked her chores with fierce determination, scrubbing the floors until her knuckles bled and gathering twice as much kindling as usual from the beach. If she worked harder, perhaps she could earn her keep.

But the whispers continued. At church on Sunday, Eva felt the weight of sideways glances and abruptly ended conversations. Mrs Turnbull, the baker's wife who had once slipped Eva extra biscuits, now shook her head sadly when she thought Eva wasn't looking.

"Poor Gemma Fisher," Eva overheard her telling another woman. "Heart bigger than her purse, that one. Taking in a shipwreck orphan when she can barely feed herself."

"The girl should be in the workhouse," came the reply. "It's where orphans belong."

The word "workhouse" sent a chill through Eva that had nothing to do with the December air. She'd heard whispers about such places—children working from dawn till dusk, thin gruel for meals, beatings for the smallest infractions.

That evening, Mrs Fisher sat Eva down by the fire after their meagre supper of fish soup and hard bread.

"Eva, love," she began, her weathered hands twisting in her apron. "We need to have a difficult conversation."

Eva nodded, her throat suddenly tight. She'd been expecting this.

"The winter's set to be harsh this year. The catches are poor, and prices for everything has risen." Mrs Fisher's eyes were sorrowful. "I've tried everything, but my savings are gone. I can't—" Her voice broke. "I can't afford to keep us both fed and warm through winter."

"I could work more," Eva offered desperately. "I could clean for other families, or mend nets for the fishermen—"

Mrs Fisher shook her head. "You're but eight years old, child. And no one has extra to pay for help now." She reached for Eva's hand. "I've written to the parish officials. They say there's no choice but the Middleford Workhouse."

Eva felt as though she were drowning all over again, water filling her lungs and darkness closing in. "Please," she whispered. "I don't want to go."

"Oh, my dear girl." Mrs Fisher pulled her close. "If there were any other way ... I've asked everyone. But times are hard for all, and I'm just a fisherman's widow with nothing to offer but what little I have."

That night, Eva clutched her mother's doll to her chest and prayed fervently for a miracle—for her father to appear at the door, for a distant relative to claim her, for anything but the workhouse.

The miracle didn't come. Instead, three days later, a sharp knock rattled the cottage door.

Mrs Fisher opened it to reveal a tall, imposing man with cold grey eyes and a permanent scowl etched into his fleshy face. He wore a dark coat that seemed too tight across his substantial middle, and a chain of office hung importantly around his neck.

"Mrs Fisher?" His voice matched his appearance—hard and unwelcoming.

"Yes, Mr Mountforth." Mrs Fisher's voice had gone small. "Please, come in."

Eva shrank back against the wall as the man ducked through the doorway. His gaze swept the cottage dismissively before landing on her.

"So this is the child." It wasn't a question. He approached Eva with heavy steps, looking her up and down as if assessing livestock. "Hmm. Seems healthy enough."

"Eva is a good girl," Mrs Fisher said quickly. "Very bright and hardworking."

Mr Mountforth's thin lips curved into what might have been intended as a smile but looked more like a grimace. "Good. We value industrious children at Middleford." He turned back to Mrs Fisher. "The parish has reviewed your situation and determined the child must be remanded to the workhouse, effective immediately."

"Immediately?" Mrs Fisher's face paled. "But surely she could stay until morning? It's nearly dark—"

"My time is valuable, Mrs Fisher." His tone suggested hers was not. "I've other business in the next village tomorrow. The girl comes now."

Eva clutched her doll tighter, her heart pounding. Mrs Fisher looked stricken but nodded slowly.

"Very well. Let me help her gather her things."

"No need for that." Mr Mountforth waved a dismissive hand. "Workhouse provides all necessities. Personal items are not permitted."

Eva's fingers tightened around her doll. "This was my mother's," she said, finding her voice at last. "Please, sir."

Mr Mountforth's cold eyes narrowed. "Workhouse rules, girl. Learn them now." He reached for the doll.

Mrs Fisher stepped between them. "Mr Mountforth, surely one small keepsake—"

"Sentimentality breeds contempt," he snapped. "The sooner she accepts her station, the better." His large hand closed around the doll and yanked it from Eva's grip.

"No!" Eva cried, lunging forward.

Mr Mountforth held the doll high, examining it with distaste. "Filthy thing. Probably carries disease." He tucked it into his coat pocket. "I'll dispose of it properly."

Eva felt tears burning her eyes but refused to let them fall. She wouldn't give this horrible man the satisfaction.

Mrs Fisher knelt before her, taking Eva's small hands in her own. "Listen to me," she whispered fiercely. "You are Evangeline

Hartwell, daughter of Captain Thomas Hartwell. You are brave and clever and kind. Remember who you are, no matter what happens."

Eva nodded, memorising Mrs Fisher's face—the kind eyes, the weather-lined cheeks, the gentle mouth now trembling with emotion.

"Time to go," Mr Mountforth announced impatiently. "Say your goodbyes."

Mrs Fisher embraced Eva tightly, pressing something small and hard into her palm. "Hide this," she breathed into Eva's ear. "Keep it safe."

Then she was being led away, Mr Mountforth's beefy hand clamped around her arm. Eva looked back once to see Mrs Fisher standing in the doorway, a solitary figure framed by the warm light of the cottage that had briefly been home.

In her closed fist, Eva clutched the small object Mrs Fisher had given her—a brass button from her husband's fishing coat. Not much, but something to hold onto in the darkness ahead.

BEHIND GREY WALLS

The journey to Middleford Workhouse stretched through the gathering dusk. Eva trudged beside Mr Mountforth, his grip occasionally tightening whenever her pace slowed. They travelled in silence, save for his occasional grunt of disapproval at something—the weather, the road, or perhaps Eva's very existence.

As they crested the final hill, Eva's breath caught in her throat. There it stood—a massive structure of weathered grey stone, windows barred like prison cells, surrounded by high walls that promised no escape. Chimney stacks belched thin wisps of smoke into the darkening sky. No trees softened its edges, no gardens brightened its approach. It was as if the earth itself had rejected any attempt at beauty or comfort.

"Middleford," Mr Mountforth announced with something like pride. "Your new home."

Home. The word felt wrong, a lie. This place could never be home.

They approached the iron gates, which creaked open at Mr Mountforth's command. A sour-faced woman with tightly pinned hair awaited them in the courtyard.

"Another one, Mr Mountforth?" she asked, eyeing Eva with disinterest.

"Parish case. Fisher woman couldn't keep her." He shoved Eva forward. "Name's Eva. Shipwreck orphan."

"Evangeline Hartwell," Eva corrected quietly. "Daughter of Captain Thomas Hartwell."

Mr Mountforth's hand clamped painfully on her shoulder. "You're workhouse property now, girl. Best forget fancy names and stories."

The woman—Mrs Beasley, Eva would later learn—led her through heavy wooden doors into a cavernous entrance hall. The smell hit Eva first—a mixture of boiled cabbage, lye soap, and something else, something sour like fear and despair.

"Girls' dormitory is upstairs," Mrs Beasley said. "You'll be assigned duties in the morning."

As they walked, Eva glimpsed children—hollow-eyed and thin—scurrying about with mops and buckets. None looked up. None spoke. The silence pressed against her ears, broken only by distant coughing and the occasional barked order from an adult.

The dormitory held two rows of narrow iron beds with thin mattresses. A single window, barred and set high in the wall, allowed a meagre rectangle of fading light.

"You'll sleep there," Mrs Beasley pointed to an empty bed. "Wash basin's at the end. No talking after lights out."

She departed without another word, leaving Eva standing alone among strangers. Girls of various ages sat or lay on their beds, watching her with wary eyes.

"Hello," Eva ventured. No one responded.

That night, curled on her hard mattress, Eva clutched the brass button hidden in her palm and silently wept for the warmth of Mrs Fisher's cottage, for her father's strong arms, for her mother's gentle touch—for everything lost.

Morning arrived with a clanging bell and shouted

commands. Eva was thrust into the workhouse routine—rising before dawn, cold water washing, thin gruel for breakfast, then work. Always work.

For Eva, it was the laundry. Massive tubs of scalding water, caustic soap that burned her hands raw, endless piles of sheets and clothing. Her back ached, her fingers blistered, but complaints earned only sharp rebukes or worse.

Days blurred together in a haze of exhaustion and hunger. Eva learned the unspoken rules quickly—keep your head down, work without rest, never question authority. Mr Mountforth stalked the corridors like a predator, his cane ready to strike any child deemed lazy or disobedient.

"Stand straight when I address you!" he bellowed at a small boy who couldn't stop coughing. The cane whistled through the air, landing with a crack against the child's legs. The boy bit his lip until it bled, refusing to cry out.

Eva watched, horror mingling with fury in her chest. That night, she found the boy—Charlie, barely six years old—huddled in his bed, silent tears tracking through the grime on his face.

"Does it hurt terribly?" she whispered, sitting beside him.

He nodded, eyes wide with surprise at her kindness.

"My father was a sea captain," Eva told him softly. "He said brave sailors sometimes cry when they're hurt, but they never give up. You're very brave, Charlie."

A ghost of a smile touched his lips.

The following evening, Eva gathered Charlie and several other young children in a shadowy corner of the dormitory after work hours.

"I'll tell you a story," she promised. "About a ship called the Lydia and the stars that guide sailors home."

Their faces—dirty, thin, and bruised—lit up with wonder as she described the vast ocean, the constellations William had taught her, and her father's courage during the storm.

"Are you really a captain's daughter?" a little girl named Betsy asked.

"I am," Eva said firmly. "And you know what? Before I came here, I was going to be a teacher."

"Could you teach us things?" Charlie asked eagerly.

Eva glanced toward the door, then nodded. "I could teach you letters. Would you like that?"

And so began Eva's secret school. Each night, after the workhouse fell silent, she gathered the youngest children. Using a stick in the thin layer of dust on the floor, she traced letters, teaching them to read words. She invented counting games using buttons and pebbles smuggled from the yard. When the dust was wiped away, no evidence remained of their forbidden education.

"Remember," she whispered to them, "knowing things is power. They can take away everything else, but not what's in your mind."

For the first time since arriving at Middleford, Eva felt purpose. In the grey darkness of the workhouse, she created a tiny flame of hope—not just for the children, but for herself. Each night, before sleep claimed her, Eva pressed Mrs Fisher's brass button to her lips like a talisman and whispered her true name: "Evangeline Hartwell, daughter of Captain Thomas Hartwell."

No matter what Mr Mountforth claimed, she would not forget who she was.

SILENT REBELLION

*E*ight years passed within Middleford's grey walls. Eva's childhood slipped away, replaced by the hardened resilience of a young woman who had known little but labour and deprivation. Yet something else emerged from this chrysalis of suffering—a beauty that couldn't be dimmed by threadbare clothes or the pallor of too little sunlight.

At sixteen, Eva's golden curls cascaded down her back when unbound, catching what little light filtered through the high windows. Her blue eyes, though shadowed by exhaustion, retained their brightness—like fragments of sky in the colourless world of the workhouse.

This transformation did not go unnoticed.

"Evangeline," Mr Mountforth's voice carried across the laundry room one afternoon. He rarely used her full name, preferring to bark out "girl" or "Hartwell" when addressing her.

Eva's hands stilled in the wash water. The other girls kept their heads down, shoulders hunched, as if trying to make themselves invisible.

"Sir?" She straightened, wiping her raw hands on her apron.

Mr Mountforth approached, his boots clicking on the stone

floor. "Your work has been most satisfactory these past months." His gaze lingered on her face, then drifted lower. "Most satisfactory indeed."

"Thank you, sir." Eva kept her voice neutral, though her skin crawled.

"Such a pretty face shouldn't be hidden away in the laundry forever." He reached out, catching a loose strand of her hair between his fingers. "Perhaps it's time we found more ... suitable duties for you."

Eva stepped back, bumping against the washtub. "I'm quite content with my current position, sir."

His smile didn't reach his eyes. "Content? No one should be content in a workhouse, girl. Ambition is what separates the worthy from the worthless."

That evening, Eva gathered her young charges in their usual corner. Charlie, now fourteen, sat closest to her. The others—Betsy, Samuel, and little Mary—huddled around, their faces solemn in the dim light.

"Something's wrong," Charlie whispered. "You look frightened."

Eva forced a smile. "Not frightened. Cautious. There's a difference."

"Is it Mr Mountforth?" Betsy asked. "He watches you different now."

Eva hesitated, then nodded. "Which is why tonight's lesson is especially important." She traced a word in the dust: COURAGE.

"Courage," Samuel read proudly.

"Yes. Courage isn't about never feeling afraid. It's about facing what frightens you with your head held high." Eva looked at each child in turn. "Remember who you are. No matter what anyone tells you, no matter how they treat you—they cannot take away your true self unless you let them."

The following morning, Eva overheard Mr Mountforth

speaking with Mrs Beasley in the corridor outside the dining hall.

"—been considering my position," he was saying. "A man of my standing ought to have a wife, wouldn't you agree?"

"Certainly, sir." Mrs Beasley's tone was deferential. "Though suitable matches are hard to come by in these parts."

"Perhaps not as hard as you might think." His voice lowered. "That Hartwell girl has grown into quite the beauty. With proper guidance, she could be moulded into something presentable."

"The workhouse girl?" Mrs Beasley sounded shocked. "But surely—"

"She has education beyond her station. I've heard her speaking to the younger inmates—quite the vocabulary for a pauper. With the right handling ..."

Eva backed away, her heart hammering against her ribs. The threat wasn't just in his words but in the calculating tone—as if she were merely another asset to be managed, another possession to be claimed.

That night, her lesson changed. While the younger children slept, Eva gathered the older ones—those approaching the age when they might be sent out as apprentices or servants.

"We must be prepared," she told them, her voice barely above a whisper. "For what awaits beyond these walls, yes, but also for what threatens us within them."

"You mean Mr Mountforth," said Charlie. It wasn't a question.

Eva nodded. "He sees us as property, not people. But we know differently, don't we?"

They nodded solemnly.

"Each night, I've taught you letters and numbers. But the most important lesson is this: your worth isn't determined by what others say about you. My father taught me that we're all born with a light inside us." Eva placed her hand over her heart.

"Some try to extinguish that light through cruelty or fear. Our task is to protect it."

"How?" asked Betsy, her thin face serious in the shadows.

"By remembering who we are. By helping each other. By refusing to become what they believe us to be." Eva reached out, taking their hands in hers. "Promise me you'll remember, no matter what happens."

"We promise," they whispered in unison.

Eva squeezed their hands, her resolve hardening like steel tempered in fire. Mr Mountforth might see her as a possession to be claimed, but she was Captain Hartwell's daughter. She would not be broken, and she would not allow these children—her children now, in all the ways that mattered—to be broken either.

In the darkest corner of Middleford Workhouse, a silent rebellion took root, nourished by the stubborn hope that even here, love and dignity could survive.

INFERNO

*E*va jolted awake to screams. Not the usual night terrors that plagued the workhouse dormitories, but something different—something urgent. The air felt wrong, thick and acrid. Her eyes snapped open to an orange glow flickering against the ceiling.

Fire.

She bolted upright, heart hammering against her ribs. Smoke billowed through the doorway, dark and choking. Children scrambled from their beds in panic, some still half-asleep, others frozen in terror.

"Everyone up!" Eva's voice cut through the chaos. "Cover your mouths with your nightgowns!"

Little Mary clutched her blanket, eyes wide with fear. "Miss Eva, I'm scared!"

Eva crossed the room in three strides, scooping Mary into her arms. "I know, love. But remember what we practiced? The drills?"

The children had never seen a proper fire drill, of course—Mountforth considered such things a waste of time. But Eva had insisted on teaching them anyway, whispering instructions during their secret lessons.

"Charlie!" Eva called to the boy who'd grown tall despite years of meager rations. "Take Samuel's hand. Betsy, gather the little ones by the far wall."

The smoke thickened, stinging her eyes. Through the haze, Eva counted heads—twelve children in this dormitory alone. She knew there were at least forty more scattered throughout the building.

"Listen to me," Eva commanded, her voice steady despite the fear clawing at her throat. "Stay low where the air is clearer. We're going to form a chain, just like we practiced. Each older child responsible for a younger one."

A thunderous crash echoed from below—part of the kitchen ceiling collapsing, Eva guessed. They had minutes, not hours.

"Charlie, you'll lead. Remember the back staircase? The one the laundry girls use?"

Charlie nodded, his face smudged with soot but determined. "Past the linen cupboard, down to the yard."

"Perfect." Eva squeezed his shoulder. "I'll bring up the rear after checking the other dormitories."

Betsy grabbed Eva's sleeve. "But Mr Mountforth said we're never to use that staircase!"

"Mr Mountforth isn't here," Eva replied, her voice hardening. "And his rules won't save us now."

Eva positioned Mary on Charlie's back, the little girl's arms wrapped tightly around his neck. She organized the remaining children into pairs, each older child clutching the hand of a younger one.

"Keep low, follow Charlie, and don't stop for anything," Eva instructed. "I'll be right behind you after I check on the others."

As the children formed their line, Eva darted into the corridor. The main staircase was already engulfed in flames, crackling and spitting as the old wood fed the fire. Heat blasted her face as she turned toward the boys' dormitory.

Inside, chaos reigned. Two older boys were attempting to corral the younger ones, but panic had taken hold. A small boy cowered under his bed, refusing to move.

"Samuel!" Eva dropped to her knees beside the bed. "Samuel, we must go now."

"I can't," he whimpered. "The fire will get me."

Eva reached under the bed, grasping his trembling hands. "The fire will only get you if you stay here. I promise I won't let go of you."

His tear-streaked face emerged from the shadows. "Promise?"

"Captain Hartwell's daughter never breaks a promise," Eva said firmly, pulling him into her arms.

With Samuel clutching her neck, Eva directed the remaining boys to join Charlie's group in the corridor. The heat intensified, sweat streaming down her face as she counted heads once more.

"The little ones from the nursery," a boy named Jacob reminded her. "They're still upstairs!"

Eva's stomach lurched. The nursery—where the youngest children slept under the supervision of ancient Mrs Pratt, who was nearly deaf. Would they have heard the commotion?

"Take them down now," Eva instructed Jacob, passing Samuel to him. "Follow the others. I'll get the nursery."

The smoke grew denser as Eva fought her way up the narrow back staircase. Flames licked at the banisters, consuming the dry wood with frightening speed. The nursery door was shut tight—a small mercy that had kept the worst of the smoke at bay.

Inside, Mrs Pratt lay slumped in her chair, overcome by the fumes that had seeped under the door. Five small children huddled together in a corner, wide-eyed and silent with terror.

"Come, little ones," Eva called, her voice hoarse from the smoke. "We're going on an adventure."

She roused Mrs Pratt with difficulty, supporting the elderly woman with one arm while gathering the smallest child with the other. The remaining four formed a chain, each clutching the nightgown of the child in front.

The journey down the stairs was a nightmare of heat and darkness. Twice, Eva nearly stumbled as pieces of burning debris fell around them. Mrs Pratt wheezed and coughed, her weight growing heavier with each step.

When they finally reached the ground floor, Eva's lungs burned, her vision blurring at the edges. The rear exit loomed ahead, a rectangle of blessed darkness beyond the inferno.

"Almost there," Eva gasped, urging the children forward. "Just a few more steps."

They burst through the door into the cool night air, gulping it greedily. Eva lowered Mrs Pratt onto the grass before counting the nursery children one final time. All present.

In the yard, Charlie had organized the others into groups, the older children comforting the younger ones. Eva's heart swelled with fierce pride even as exhaustion threatened to overwhelm her.

Villagers were arriving now, alerted by the glow on the horizon. Some formed bucket chains from the well, though their efforts seemed pitiful against the raging inferno. Others wrapped blankets around shivering children.

As dawn broke, Eva stood watching the flames consume the workhouse that had been her prison for eight long years. The building that had witnessed her transformation from a frightened child to a young woman groaned and cracked as its beams surrendered to the fire.

"You saved them," a voice said beside her. Eva turned to find Charlie, his face streaked with soot and tears. "You saved all of us."

Eva looked across the yard at the children—her children—huddled together but alive. Free.

"No," she said softly. "WE saved each other."

FREEDOM'S PATH

Daylight fully emerged, illuminating the smoking ruins of Middleford Workhouse. Parish officials arrived with constables, attempting to gather the scattered children into orderly groups. Eva watched from the edge of the crowd as Mr Mountforth gesticulated wildly, his face contorted with rage as he pointed at the children, then at the building.

"Arson!" he bellowed. "Someone will hang for this!"

His gaze swept the yard, landing on Eva. Something in his expression chilled her blood—recognition, calculation, hatred. He started toward her, shoving children aside.

Eva backed away, bumping into Charlie.

"You need to go," he whispered urgently. "He'll blame you for everything."

"I can't leave you all—"

"You must." Charlie's young face looked suddenly older, determined. "We'll be all right. The constables won't let him hurt us now that everyone's watching."

Villagers swarmed forward with blankets and offers of temporary shelter, creating a chaotic scene of movement and noise. Eva felt Charlie's small hand press something into hers—a few coins.

"Nicked them from Mountforth's office before it went up," he admitted with a fleeting grin. "Better use than lining his pockets."

Eva pulled Charlie into a fierce embrace. "Take care of the little ones if you can."

"I will. Remember what you taught us—we're not just workhouse property."

The crowd surged as more officials arrived, separating them. Eva caught glimpses of familiar faces—Samuel being led away by a farmer's wife, Betsy clutching Mary's hand as they followed a parish woman, Jacob helping the youngest children into a cart. In moments, they vanished among the throng of adults taking charge.

Eva's throat tightened. These children had become her family, her purpose. Now they scattered like dandelion seeds in the wind, their futures unknown. She closed her eyes briefly, whispering a prayer.

"Lord, watch over them. Keep them safe from those who would harm them. Let them remember they are worthy of love."

When she opened her eyes, Mountforth was pushing through the crowd toward her, pointing and shouting. Two constables turned in her direction.

It was time.

Eva slipped behind a cluster of villagers and darted toward the road. Her legs carried her swiftly away from the only place she'd known for eight years, each step both terrifying and exhilarating. She didn't look back.

The morning sun warmed her face as she walked briskly along the country lane. London—that was where she would go. William had spoken of it with such wonder during those precious days aboard the SS Lydia. A place large enough to disappear in, with opportunities for those willing to work.

Eva's hand slipped into her pocket, fingers finding Mrs Fisher's brass button and Charlie's stolen coins—her entire fortune.

The road stretched before her, winding through rolling green hills dotted with sheep. Eva had no map, no plan beyond putting distance between herself and Middleford. She would follow the sun, ask directions when necessary, and trust that each step took her closer to freedom.

By midday, hunger gnawed at her stomach. Eva stopped beside a clear stream to drink and rest her aching feet. The water reflected her image—soot-streaked face, tangled hair, eyes bright with a mixture of fear and determination. She barely recognised herself.

"Captain Hartwell's daughter," she whispered to her reflection, remembering Mrs Fisher's words. "That's who I am."

The journey proved more challenging than Eva had anticipated. She walked until her feet blistered, then walked more. Villages appeared on the horizon, then fell behind her. Sometimes she accepted rides on farmers' carts, offering to help with their loads in exchange. Other times she walked alone for hours, the vast countryside both beautiful and intimidating in its emptiness.

At night, she slept in barns when she could find them, or under hedgerows when she couldn't. The spring air carried a chill after sunset that seeped into her bones. Eva huddled beneath her thin workhouse dress, clutching Mrs Fisher's button tight in her fist for comfort.

"I will find a new life," she promised herself each morning as she rose stiff and cold. "I will be more than what they tried to make me."

On the fourth day, the landscape began to change. Villages grew larger, closer together. More travellers appeared on the road, carts laden with goods bound for market. And in the distance, a haze hung over the horizon—not the clean mist of the countryside, but the smoke of countless chimneys.

London awaited.

LONDON

*E*va paused at the crest of Blackheath Hill, her breath catching at the sprawling vista before her. London unfurled like a vast living creature, stretching farther than her eyes could see. Countless spires and chimneys pierced the sky, while the great snake of the Thames River wound through the city's heart.

The distant tolling of church bells mingled with the rumble of carriages and carts. Even from this distance, the city's pulse was palpable—relentless, indifferent, alive.

"So this is London," she whispered. The enormity of what lay ahead suddenly pressed upon her. In Middleford, despite its cruelties, she'd known her place and purpose. Here, she was but one small soul among thousands.

Eva straightened her shoulders. "Well," she murmured to herself, "we've come this far. No turning back now."

With each step toward the city, the noise grew louder, the air thicker with coal smoke and the mingled odours of humanity. By the time Eva reached the first proper streets, her senses reeled from the assault. Vendors shouted their wares, children darted between carts, gentlemen in fine coats brushed past women in elaborate dresses. Dogs barked, horses neighed, wheels clattered on cobblestones.

A passing carriage splashed through a puddle, spraying dirty water across Eva's already filthy dress. No one stopped to notice the bedraggled girl with soot-stained cheeks. No one cared.

The realisation struck her with unexpected force. In Middleford, she'd been watched constantly, her every movement scrutinised and judged. Here, she was invisible—terrifying yet oddly liberating.

Eva wandered deeper into the labyrinth of streets, disoriented by the constant flow of humanity. Her stomach growled painfully. When had she last eaten? Yesterday morning, a crust of bread offered by a kind farmer's wife.

The coins in her pocket wouldn't last long. She needed shelter, food, work—but where to begin?

A flash of green caught her eye. Through a gap between buildings, she glimpsed trees. Following the sight, Eva found herself at the edge of a small park. Not grand or manicured like those William had described, but a modest square of grass and trees surrounded by iron railings.

Eva slipped through the gate and sank onto a bench, her legs trembling with exhaustion. The relative quiet washed over her like a balm. Here, the city's roar diminished to a distant rumble. The sweet scent of early spring flowers replaced the stench of sewage and unwashed bodies.

She closed her eyes, breathing deeply. "What now, Lord?" she whispered. Her mother's faith had always guided her through darkness. "I'm alone in this great city. Show me the way forward."

When she opened her eyes, a small cluster of daisies caught her attention, growing stubbornly through a crack in the paving stones. Eva smiled at their persistence. Reaching down, she gently plucked them, arranging them into a tiny bouquet.

The flowers reminded her of quiet afternoons with Mrs

Fisher, learning to weave fishing nets. The same principle applied to stems and petals. Eva's fingers worked deftly, muscle memory guiding them as she twisted the delicate stems together.

"Pretty flowers for a pretty lady?"

Eva startled at the voice. A well-dressed woman stood before her, gloved hand extended toward the daisies.

"I—I wasn't—" Eva stammered, suddenly aware of how she must appear—dirty, dishevelled, stealing flowers from a public park.

The woman's expression softened. "No need for alarm, child. I merely wondered if those were for sale. They're arranged so charmingly."

Eva looked down at the small bouquet in her hands. "Would you like them?"

"How much?"

Eva hesitated, having no notion of London prices. "Whatever you think fair, ma'am."

The woman extracted a penny from her purse. "Will this do?"

A whole penny for a few daisies! Eva nodded, carefully handing over her creation.

"You have a gift for arrangement," the woman remarked, admiring the simple bouquet. "Good day to you."

As the woman walked away, Eva stared at the copper coin in her palm. An idea bloomed in her mind, bright as the daisies she'd just sold.

By sunset, Eva had sold six more small bouquets, gathering wildflowers from the park's edges and arranging them with care. Each transaction built her confidence. She'd earned enough for a hot meat pie from a street vendor, the first proper meal she'd had in days.

Night fell, bringing with it new concerns. Where would she

sleep? The park gates would close, and she dared not risk the streets after dark.

Eva eventually found shelter in the doorway of a closed shop, huddled against the wall. Sleep came fitfully, disturbed by passing drunks and the occasional constable's whistle.

Morning brought stiff limbs but renewed determination. Eva washed her face and hands at a public pump, then combed her fingers through her tangled hair. She couldn't sell flowers looking like a beggar girl.

Eva smoothed her threadbare dress and squared her shoulders. The needle and thread she'd purchased with yesterday's flower earnings felt like old friends in her pocket. At Middleford, mending had been endless drudgery—now it might be her salvation.

She positioned herself near a busy market street, watching the flow of people. A gentleman passed with a torn sleeve barely concealed beneath his coat. A woman hurried by, the hem of her dress dragging and frayed.

"Mending done quick and neat," Eva called, her voice stronger than she felt. "Finest stitching, reasonable rates."

The first few people brushed past without acknowledgment. Eva's heart sank but she persisted, remembering her father's words about perseverance.

"Excuse me, miss " Eva approached a harried-looking woman juggling a basket of vegetables and a squirming toddler. "I couldn't help but notice your son's jacket needs repair. I could mend it properly by tomorrow morning."

The woman paused, eyeing Eva suspiciously. "You're awfully young to be a seamstress."

"I've been sewing since I was six years old," Eva replied

truthfully. She extended her hand, revealing callused fingertips. "These aren't the hands of someone who's afraid of work."

Something in Eva's steady gaze must have convinced the woman. "Very well. What would you charge?"

"Tuppence for the jacket, and I'll throw in fixing that loose button on your sleeve."

The transaction complete, Eva worked diligently through the afternoon, sitting in the same park where she'd sold flowers. Her needle flashed in the sunlight as she executed perfect, tiny stitches on the boy's jacket.

Two more customers followed—an elderly man with torn pockets and a young maid whose Sunday dress needed hemming. Eva treated each garment with respect, regardless of its quality, just as she maintained her own dignity despite her circumstances.

As dusk approached, a girl selling matches passed by, eyeing Eva's work.

"You're new," she observed bluntly. "Where'd you learn to sew like that?"

"My mother taught me the basics," Eva replied, tying off a neat row of stitches. "I refined my skills elsewhere."

The girl nodded toward Eva's small pile of mending. "Better than selling matches, that. You got somewhere to sleep tonight?"

Eva hesitated. "Not exactly."

"Thought not. There's a place near the bakery on Clarendon Road. They don't mind girls sleeping in the alley if you're quiet and gone before the owner wakes."

Eva met the girl's eyes. "Thank you. I'm Eva."

"Lucy." The girl shifted her matches to her other hand. "Word of advice, Eva. Keep your chin up like you're doing, but watch your back. London eats the weak alive."

CITY LIFE

*E*va wiped down the sticky wooden table, wringing her cloth into a bucket of murky water. The Whistling Sailor tavern hummed with conversation, pipe smoke hanging thick in the air. After two weeks of flower selling and mending, she'd discovered that taverns paid better—though the work demanded stronger nerves.

"Another round for my friends!" A merchant slapped coins onto Eva's tray. "And be quick about it, pretty one."

"Right away, sir." Eva tucked the coins safely into her apron pocket before weaving between crowded tables toward the bar.

Mr Finch, the tavern owner, poured three pints with practiced efficiency. "You're earning your keep, girl. The men like a fresh face."

"Thank you for the opportunity, sir." Eva balanced the drinks carefully on her tray. Several patrons had already offered her "better work" with sly winks and wandering hands. She'd learned to sidestep these advances with a polite firmness that discouraged without offending.

"God helps those who help themselves," she whispered to herself, a phrase her mother had often repeated. Eva had taken to reciting these fragments of her past like prayers, keeping the memories alive.

When she returned to the merchant's table, one of his companions grabbed her wrist.

"What's your story then, love? Heard that American twang in your voice. That is an exciting story for certain!"

Eva gently extracted her arm. "My story is quite ordinary, sir. I'm simply grateful for honest work."

The man's companion laughed. "Leave the girl be, Howard. Can't you see she's not that sort?"

Eva moved away, grateful for the intervention. Not all customers were predatory—some reminded her of her father, decent men simply enjoying respite after long days of labour.

"Evangeline!" Mr Finch called from behind the bar. "Kitchen needs you."

In the steamy kitchen, Eva scrubbed pots alongside Maggie, a girl barely older than herself with bright red hair and a quicker tongue.

"Men giving you trouble?" Maggie asked, attacking a burnt pot with vigour.

"Nothing I can't handle."

"Just be careful, because winter's coming. Sleeping rough gets harder when frost sets in." Maggie glanced at Eva's thin shawl. "Some of us meet behind the chandler's shop after closing. Safety in numbers and all that. You should join."

Later that night, Eva followed Maggie to a small courtyard where several young people huddled around a meagre fire in an old barrel. Lucy the match girl was there, along with two boys who sold newspapers and a hollow-cheeked girl Eva recognised from the market.

"This is Eva," Maggie announced. "She's new but clever with a needle."

The group chuckled, making room for Eva in their circle.

Tom, the older newspaper boy, offered her a potato baked in the embers.

"Where'd you sleep last night?" he asked. "Places here gets dangerous after midnight."

"I found a doorway on Paxton Street," Eva admitted. "The shopkeeper chased me off at dawn."

"We've a better spot," said Jenny, the market girl. "Warehouse on Blackstock Road. Owner doesn't mind as long as we're gone before his workers arrive. Even has a water pump round back."

As the night deepened, they shared stories of their days—coins earned, troubles avoided, small victories celebrated. Eva listened, offering mending tips when Jenny complained about her torn stockings.

"You talk different," observed the younger newspaper boy, Billy. "You aren't from round here are you?"

Eva hesitated. "I come from Boston. My father was a sea captain."

"Where's he now then?" Billy asked innocently.

The circle fell silent at the tactless question.

"Lost at sea," Eva replied softly. "Near Liverpool, almost two years ago now."

Maggie squeezed her hand. "My da was crushed in the dockyard. Life's cruel that way."

One by one, they shared their losses—parents claimed by fever, accidents, or simply vanished into London's vastness. Their stories echoed Eva's own, creating an unexpected kinship in shared grief.

When the others finally dozed off, Eva remained awake, watching the dying embers.

"I miss you," she whispered to the embers, imagining her words reaching her parents somehow. "I'm trying to make you proud."

She'd survived the workhouse. She would survive London too.

Days blended into weeks, then months. Eva established a routine—mending in mornings, tavern work evenings, sleeping alongside her newfound friends at night. She saved every spare penny in a small tin hidden beneath a loose floorboard in the warehouse.

Winter arrived with biting winds that cut through her threadbare clothes. On particularly harsh nights, the group pooled resources for a room at Mrs Granger's lodging house—eight of them crammed into space meant for four, but warm nonetheless.

One bitter December evening, Eva encountered a small boy shivering in an alleyway, clutching a thin blanket.

"Where's your family?" she asked, kneeling beside him.

"Gone," he replied through chattering teeth. "Fever took 'em."

Without hesitation, Eva shared her bread and led him to the warehouse. "I know what it's like to be alone," she told him. "But you needn't be tonight."

"Why help me?" the boy asked suspiciously.

Eva thought of Charlie, who'd given her his stolen coins; of Mrs Fisher, who'd taken her in despite her own poverty; of her father, who'd helped others even as the ship sank beneath him.

"Because kindness matters," she replied simply. "Especially when the world seems unkind."

By spring, Eva had established herself as something of a leader among the street children. Her mending business grew steadily, with some customers specifically seeking "the girl with the golden hair and neat stitches." Mr Finch promoted her from cleaning to serving, appreciating her ability to handle difficult patrons with grace.

On her seventeenth birthday—a date no one else knew—Eva treated herself to a moment alone in St Paul's Cathedral. Sitting in a quiet corner, she opened her palm to reveal Mrs Fisher's brass button.

"I've survived another year," she whispered to the talismans of her past. "I won't always live like this. Someday, I'll have a proper home again." She closed her eyes, remembering her father's voice, her mother's gentle hands. "I won't forget who I am. Evangeline Hartwell. Daughter of Captain Thomas Hartwell. And I will make something of myself in this city, I promise you both."

A NEW CHAPTER

Summer sunshine warmed Eva's shoulders as she walked along Bond Street, delivering a mended cloak to Mrs Ward. The lady had paid her handsomely—three shillings!—for repairing delicate lace trim. Eva clutched the coins in her pocket, already calculating how many meals they would buy.

A glimmer caught her eye. Across the street stood a modest dress shop, its window displaying a gown of pale blue silk. Sunlight danced across pearl buttons and fine embroidery. Eva stopped, transfixed by the craftsmanship.

A small sign in flowing script read: "Thornton's Fine Dressmaking & Alterations."

Eva's heart quickened. Just yesterday, she'd prayed for direction, feeling increasingly restless with her precarious existence. Could this be an answer?

"It's worth trying," she whispered to herself, smoothing her worn but clean dress. She crossed the street before courage deserted her.

A small bell tinkled as Eva pushed open the door. The shop interior smelled of lavender and fresh fabric. Bolts of cotton, silk, and wool lined shelves along one wall. A counter displayed ribbons, buttons, and lace samples. Two dressmaker's forms stood by the window, one draped with the blue silk gown, the other with a half-finished emerald creation.

"Good afternoon. May I help you?"

A woman emerged from the back room, pins tucked in the sleeve of her sensible brown dress. She appeared to be in her late thirties, with dark hair neatly arranged in a bun. Soft grey eyes regarded Eva with polite curiosity.

"Good afternoon, ma'am." Eva curtseyed slightly. "I—I noticed your beautiful work in the window."

The woman smiled, her expression warming. "Thank you, dear. I'm Miss Adelaide Thornton. Are you looking for a dress?"

Eva glanced down at her mended garment. "No, ma'am. I... I'm a seamstress. I've been doing mending work around London, but I've always dreamed of working with fine dresses."

"You have a slight accent." Miss Thornton tilted her head, studying Eva with newfound interest. "Not quite London."

Eva's fingers twisted nervously at her skirt. "I was born in Boston, ma'am. America. My father and I came to England when I was eight." The memory of the Lydia's wooden deck beneath her feet flashed briefly. "That was many years ago now. People say the accent is fading."

"Boston," Miss Thornton repeated, as if testing the word. Her grey eyes softened. "I've heard it's quite beautiful. Almost as civilised as London, they say."

Eva smiled despite her nervousness. "The harbour there reminds me a little of the Thames."

Miss Thornton's eyebrow raised slightly. "You're a seamstress you say? And where did you learn to sew?"

"My mother taught me basics as a child. Then ..." Eva hesitated, unwilling to mention the workhouse. "I've had to make my own way these past years. I can show you my work."

From her pocket, Eva produced a handkerchief she'd

embroidered with delicate violets—a small luxury she'd created from scraps.

Miss Thornton examined it, her fingers tracing the tiny, even stitches. "This is quite fine work." She looked up, studying Eva's face. "What's your name, child?"

"Evangeline Hartwell, ma'am. Though most call me Eva."

"Miss Hartwell, my assistant left two weeks ago to marry. I've been managing alone since." She gestured to a half-finished bodice. "Would you care to show me what you can do with this?"

Eva's heart leapt. She removed her shawl and took the offered needle. Working with steady hands, she completed a row of nearly invisible stitches along the seam.

Miss Thornton watched silently, then nodded. "Very good. Now, the buttonholes?"

For twenty minutes, Eva demonstrated various techniques while Miss Thornton observed. Finally, the older woman smiled.

"Miss Hartwell, I believe you have a natural gift. I'd like to offer you a position—six shillings weekly to start, with room for advancement as you learn. There's a small chamber above the shop you may use, if you need accommodation."

Eva's hands trembled. "Truly?"

"I trust my instincts about people," Miss Thornton said simply. "Something tells me you were meant to walk through that door today."

"Thank you, Miss Thornton. I'll work hard, I promise." Eva fought back tears of relief. "When shall I begin?"

"Tomorrow morning, eight o'clock sharp. Tonight, gather your belongings." Miss Thornton hesitated. "Do you have family to inform?"

"No family, ma'am. But I should say goodbye to some friends who've been kind to me."

That evening, Eva hurried to the warehouse on Blackstock Road. Her friends gathered around as she shared her news.

"A proper job in a dress shop!" Maggie exclaimed. "With a room of your own!"

"We always knew you'd find something better," Tom said, punching her shoulder affectionately.

Jenny wiped away a tear. "You'll visit us, won't you?"

"Of course I will," Eva promised, embracing each one. "I wouldn't have survived without you all."

Billy, the younger newspaper boy, presented her with a slightly bruised apple. "For luck," he mumbled.

As darkness fell, they celebrated with a small feast—bread, cheese, and a bottle of ginger beer Tom had splurged on. They told stories late into the night, until it was time for Eva to leave.

Standing at the warehouse door, Eva looked back at her friends—the family she'd found in London's harsh streets.

"This isn't goodbye," she said firmly. "It's just a new chapter."

HOME

*E*va woke before dawn, light barely filtering through the small window of her new chamber above Thornton's shop. For a moment, she lay still, savouring the novelty of a proper mattress beneath her and blankets that smelled of lavender. After months of warehouse floors and doorways, the modest room felt like a palace.

She dressed quickly, eager to begin her first day. The brass button from Mrs Fisher sat on her small bedside table—a reminder of how far she'd come.

"You're early," Miss Adelaide remarked when Eva appeared in the workroom at half past seven. "Excellent. I appreciate punctuality."

"I couldn't sleep, ma'am. Too excited to begin."

Miss Adelaide's lips curved into a small smile. "Then let's not waste a moment. I'll show you our current orders."

The morning passed in a flurry of introductions—to the workroom, the cutting table, the fabric storeroom, and the front shop area where customers were received. Eva absorbed everything with keen attention, memorising where each tool belonged and how Miss Adelaide preferred things arranged.

By mid-morning, the bell above the door announced their first customer. A plump woman with an imperious manner swept in, her daughter trailing behind.

"Miss Thornton! I require a new walking dress. Something in the latest fashion—I'm attending Lady Weatherby's garden party next month and simply cannot wear last season's styles."

"Mrs Worthings, how lovely to see you." Miss Adelaide gestured toward Eva. "This is Miss Hartwell, my new assistant. She'll be helping with your measurements today."

Eva curtseyed, noting the appraising look Mrs Worthings gave her.

"American, are you?" the woman asked, hearing Eva's faint accent as she greeted them.

"Yes, ma'am. From Boston."

"Hmm. Well, I suppose your hands work the same as English ones."

Eva bit her tongue and smiled politely. "I assure you they do, ma'am."

As Eva carefully measured the woman, Miss Adelaide displayed fabric samples. The daughter, a shy girl of perhaps fourteen, watched Eva with curious eyes.

"You have gentle hands," the girl whispered when her mother was distracted by a debate over lace trimmings.

"Thank you, miss. I've found gentleness often produces the finest work."

The rest of the day unfolded in similar fashion—measuring clients, cutting patterns, and learning Miss Adelaide's system for tracking orders. By closing time, Eva's fingers were pricked and her back ached, but a warm satisfaction filled her chest.

"You did well today," Miss Adelaide said as they tidied the workroom. "Mrs Worthings is one of our most particular customers."

"Thank you for trusting me with her."

Miss Adelaide paused, studying Eva. "You've known hardship, haven't you?"

Eva stiffened slightly. "What makes you say that?"

"Your hands. They're young but show signs of rough work. And there's something in your eyes—a wariness. I recognise it because I've seen it in my own mirror."

Eva remained silent, unsure how much to reveal.

"You needn't tell me anything you don't wish to," Miss Adelaide continued. "But know that in this shop, you're safe. I judge people by their character and their work, not their past."

"Thank you," Eva whispered, blinking back sudden tears.

Miss Adelaide nodded briskly. "Now, let's have some tea before bed. Tomorrow will be just as busy."

Over the following weeks, Eva settled into a rhythm at Thornton's. Each morning began with sweeping the shop and preparing the workroom. Throughout the day, she alternated between serving customers, cutting patterns, and sewing alongside Miss Adelaide. In the evenings, they would review the day's work over tea, planning for tomorrow's tasks.

Eva quickly learned that Miss Adelaide's customers fell into distinct categories—the wealthy matrons who demanded the latest London fashions, the middle-class wives who sought quality at reasonable prices, and the occasional young bride dreaming of her perfect wedding gown.

"The secret," Miss Adelaide confided one afternoon as they worked, "is making each woman feel that her dress is the most important creation in our shop, regardless of its price."

Eva nodded, carefully pinning a sleeve. "My mother used to say that clothes should honour the person wearing them."

"A wise woman, your mother."

"She was." Eva's voice softened with memory. "She taught me to see beauty in simple things."

Miss Adelaide smiled. "That explains your talent for embellishment. I've noticed how you can transform ordinary trim into something quite extraordinary."

One rainy Tuesday, when customers were scarce, Miss Adelaide brought out fashion plates from Paris. They spent hours poring over the illustrations, discussing how each design might be adapted for their clientele.

"What if we combined these sleeves with this neckline?" Eva suggested, pointing to different images. "It would suit Mrs Thorne's figure better than either design alone."

Miss Adelaide's eyebrows rose. "That's precisely what I was thinking. You have an excellent eye, Eva."

Encouraged, Eva shared more ideas—ways to update existing dresses with new trimmings, techniques for making modestly priced fabrics appear more luxurious, and designs that flattered various body types.

"You know," Miss Adelaide said thoughtfully, "we should create a display dress for the window. Something to showcase these ideas of yours."

"Truly?" Eva's heart raced with excitement.

"Indeed. Select whatever fabrics you wish from our remnant box. Let's see what you can create."

That evening, Eva stayed late, sketching designs by candlelight. For the first time since leaving Boston, she felt truly in her element—creating beauty from mere cloth and thread.

The following week brought an unexpected surprise. As Eva arranged fabric bolts near the window, she noticed a group of young women pause outside, pointing at a walking dress she'd recently completed.

"Excuse me," one called, entering the shop. "That blue dress in your window—it's exquisite. Might I inquire about having something similar made?"

Before the month was out, three new customers had commissioned dresses based on Eva's designs. Miss Adelaide, delighted by the increased business, gave Eva a raise.

"Your talent is bringing fresh life to this shop," she said warmly. "I'm beginning to think our meeting was providential."

One evening, as they shared a pot of tea after closing, Miss Adelaide asked, "Do you ever think of returning to America?"

Eva stared into her cup. "Sometimes I wonder if my father might still be alive. If he somehow survived the shipwreck." She shook her head. "But England is my home now. And this shop—it feels like where I'm meant to be."

Miss Adelaide reached across the table, briefly squeezing Eva's hand. "Then I'm grateful the winds brought you to my door, Evangeline Hartwell."

Eva smiled, warmth spreading through her chest. After years of displacement and struggle, she'd found not just employment, but a place where her spirit could flourish. Each stitch brought her closer to the woman she was meant to become.

BIRTHDAY CELEBRATIONS

Six months passed in a rhythm of seasons that transformed London from winter's bite to summer's warm embrace. Eva's hands, once raw from workhouse laundry, now moved with confident precision across silks and satins. Her designs adorned the shop window, drawing admiring glances from passers-by and bringing new customers through Thornton's doors.

"Another order for the lavender walking dress," Eva announced one June morning, pinning a customer's measurements to her sketchbook. "That's the third this month."

Miss Adelaide looked up from her ledger with a satisfied smile. "Your eye for detail has quite captured the ladies of Mayfair. Mrs Thorne was positively effusive about the way you adjusted the bodice to flatter her figure."

Eva blushed, still unaccustomed to praise. "The design simply follows the natural lines of the body. Nothing revolutionary."

"Nonsense. Your work shows genuine artistry." Miss Adelaide closed her ledger with a decisive snap. "Which reminds me—we've been invited to provide gowns for Lady Harrington's summer garden party. It could mean significant new patronage."

The shop hummed with activity as summer progressed. Eva rose before dawn to sketch designs, worked alongside the other seamstresses through the day, and often stayed late to finish delicate embroidery that couldn't be trusted to less experienced hands. The exhaustion felt different from her workhouse days—purposeful rather than punishing.

On quiet evenings, Eva sometimes wandered to the small park where she'd once sold wildflower bouquets. She'd watch children playing, mothers chatting on benches, gentlemen tipping their hats to passing ladies. The normalcy of it all still struck her as miraculous.

One such evening in late July, Eva noticed Miss Adelaide behaving oddly—whispering with the other seamstresses, abruptly changing topics when Eva entered the workroom, and sending her on unnecessary errands.

"Is everything all right?" Eva finally asked, concerned by the secretive atmosphere.

"Perfectly fine," Miss Adelaide replied, a bit too brightly. "Though I wonder if you might deliver this package to Mrs Winters tomorrow? It's rather out of your way, but Sarah is behind on the Ellsworth commission."

Eva agreed, puzzled but willing. The errand took longer than expected, and when she returned to the shop late the following afternoon, she found it unusually quiet.

"Miss Adelaide?" she called, stepping into the darkened front room. "I've returned from Mrs Winters'."

Suddenly, the lamps flared to life. "Surprise!" voices chorused as Eva blinked in the sudden brightness.

The shop had been transformed. Colourful fabric scraps hung from the ceiling in festive garlands. The workroom table, cleared of patterns and pins, now bore a modest feast—fresh bread, cheese, sliced apples, and a small cake decorated with wildflowers.

"Happy birthday, Eva!" Miss Adelaide stepped forward, her normally composed face alight with pleasure.

Eva's hand flew to her mouth. "My birthday? But how did you know?"

"You mentioned it once, months ago," Sarah, one of the younger seamstresses, piped up. "When we were discussing the Wilton wedding date."

"We've been planning this for weeks," added Mary, another seamstress, beaming with pride at their successful surprise.

Overwhelmed, Eva looked around at the faces of these women who had become her family. Their kindness pierced through layers of protective armour she hadn't realised she still carried.

"I haven't celebrated my birthday since—" Her voice caught.

"Since before the shipwreck," Miss Adelaide finished gently. "Which is precisely why we thought it time to resume the tradition. Eighteen is a significant milestone, after all."

Miss Adelaide guided Eva to a chair at the head of the table. "Now, before we eat, I have something for you."

She presented Eva with a package wrapped in brown paper and tied with blue ribbon. "Open it."

Eva's fingers trembled as she unwrapped the gift. Inside lay a dress unlike any she'd seen before—fashionable yet practical, with a fitted bodice and graceful skirt in a rich shade of blue that reminded her of the ocean on a clear day.

"I designed it myself," Miss Adelaide said, uncharacteristically shy. "Based on those sketches you keep hidden in your journal. I thought perhaps you might wear it to Lady Harrington's garden party. You've earned the right to attend as my assistant, not merely as a seamstress."

Tears welled in Eva's eyes as she traced the fine stitching. "It's beautiful. I've never owned anything so fine."

"Try it on!" the other girls urged.

Moments later, Eva emerged from behind the dressing screen. The dress fit perfectly, highlighting her slender figure and bringing out the blue of her eyes. Her golden curls, usually confined in a practical bun, tumbled freely over her shoulders.

"You look like a proper lady," Sarah breathed.

"She looks like herself," Miss Adelaide corrected gently. "The self she was always meant to become."

Mary appeared with glasses of sweet apple cider. "A toast to Eva!"

Eva raised her glass, blinking back tears. "Thank you all. When I came to London, I had nothing but hope and determination. Now I have so much more—work that fulfils me, a place that feels like home, and people who care." She swallowed hard. "My father would be proud to see me now, I think."

"He would indeed," Miss Adelaide agreed. "To Eva—may your eighteenth year bring all the happiness you deserve."

As the evening progressed with laughter and stories, Eva slipped away briefly to the quiet of the shop's front window. The summer twilight bathed London in golden light, transforming even the ordinary street into something magical.

She pressed her hand against the cool glass, remembering the frightened girl who had arrived in this vast city with nothing but a brass button. That girl could never have imagined this moment—surrounded by friends, respected for her work, beginning to believe in possibilities beyond mere survival.

"Thank you," she whispered, a prayer meant for her parents and for whatever providence had guided her path. "I'll make you proud."

Later, as the celebration wound down and the others began clearing away the remnants of their feast, Miss Adelaide found Eva sitting quietly, running her fingers over the blue dress.

"Happy birthday, my dear," she said softly. "I hope it was everything you wished for."

Eva looked up, her face radiant with newfound certainty. "It was more than I dared wish for. And tomorrow—tomorrow I begin my eighteenth year ready to face whatever comes."

The first stars appeared in the darkening sky beyond the shop window, bright points of light guiding the way forward.

THE PEMBROKES

Morning light streamed through the windows of Thornton's Fine Dressmaking & Alterations, catching dust motes that danced above bolts of vibrant fabric. Eva pinned a sleeve to a bodice with practiced precision, her fingers moving swiftly as the shop bustled with activity around her.

"Eva, could you please finish the embroidery on Mrs Whitmore's evening gown? She'll be collecting it this afternoon," Miss Adelaide called from her workstation, where she sketched a design for a summer ball gown.

"Of course," Eva replied, setting aside her current work to retrieve the nearly completed gown from the storage room.

Summer had arrived in full force, bringing with it a flurry of orders for garden parties, evening soirées, and wedding celebrations. The bell above the door chimed incessantly as ladies of varying social standing entered to commission new pieces or collect finished garments.

The warm June air carried the sweet scent of freshly brewed tea from the pot Miss Adelaide kept brewing throughout the day. Eva had quickly learned that tea served two purposes in the shop—it refreshed the seamstresses during long hours of detailed work and it loosened the purse strings of hesitant customers.

"Would you care for another cup, Mrs Holloway?" Eva offered to a plump woman examining lace trimmings. "Perhaps while you consider the azure silk, the color and fabric would complement your complexion beautifully."

By midday, Eva's fingers ached pleasantly from hours of delicate stitching. She stretched her back, admiring the completed embroidery on Mrs Whitmore's gown—an intricate pattern of lilies that trailed along the neckline, each petal defined by Eva's meticulous hand.

A momentary lull fell over the shop as the last morning customer departed. The seamstresses exchanged relieved glances, taking the opportunity to rest briefly before the afternoon rush began.

The peaceful interlude shattered as the bell above the door chimed with particular vigour. Eva looked up to see a vision of elegance sweep into the shop—a young woman with striking auburn hair and a gown that whispered of wealth with every movement. Two maids followed in her wake, carrying parcels and parasols.

"Miss Thornton!" the woman exclaimed, her voice musical and confident. "I've come with the most urgent request."

Miss Adelaide hurried forward, her face brightening with recognition. "Lady Pembroke! What a delightful surprise."

Eva continued her work, but her ears pricked at the name. The Pembrokes were among London's elite—their name frequently appearing in society columns and whispered conversations among customers.

"I simply must have a new gown for the Harrington garden party," Lady Pembroke declared, removing her gloves with dramatic flair. "Something that will make even the flowers jealous."

Miss Adelaide laughed. "We shall endeavour to outshine nature herself. May I present some designs for your consideration?"

As Lady Pembroke followed Miss Adelaide to the design table, Eva couldn't help but observe her. Everything about the young woman exuded confidence and breeding—from her perfect posture to the way she gestured expressively while speaking. It was like watching a creature from another world, one Eva had glimpsed only through shop windows and carriage glass.

The bell chimed again, and Eva's hands faltered mid-stitch.

A gentleman entered, tall and broad-shouldered, with dark brown hair that caught the sunlight streaming through the windows. His deep blue eyes surveyed the shop with casual interest before settling on Lady Pembroke.

"Scarlett, you promised this wouldn't take long," he said, his voice rich and warm.

"James! Perfect timing," Lady Pembroke replied. "Miss Thornton is about to show me designs. You can provide a gentleman's perspective."

Eva found herself straightening her posture, smoothing her apron, and tucking a stray curl behind her ear. She kept her eyes on her work, but her awareness remained fixed on the gentleman's presence. When she dared a glance, she found him examining a bolt of emerald silk with genuine interest rather than affected boredom.

"Eva," Miss Adelaide called, "would you bring the summer pattern book and take Lady Pembroke's measurements?"

Heart fluttering, Eva gathered her tools and approached the trio. Lord Pembroke's eyes met hers briefly, and she felt a curious warmth spread across her cheeks.

"This is Miss Hartwell, my finest seamstress," Miss Adelaide introduced her. "She has quite the eye for design."

"Charmed," Lady Pembroke said with a smile that seemed genuine despite the difference in their stations.

Lord Pembroke inclined his head. "Miss Hartwell."

Eva curtseyed, then proceeded to measure Lady Pembroke with practiced efficiency, noting the numbers in her small leather-bound notebook. As she worked, she offered quiet suggestions about cuts and fabrics that might complement Lady Pembroke's colouring and figure.

"You see, brother?" Lady Pembroke turned to Lord Pembroke. "This is why I insisted on Thornton's. Such attention to detail."

Lord Pembroke watched Eva's movements with undisguised interest. "Indeed. Craftsmanship is becoming a rare quality these days."

Eva felt his gaze like warmth on her skin as she pinned a sample of lavender silk against Lady Pembroke's shoulder. "This shade brings out the amber in your eyes, my lady," she observed.

"Does it, James?" Lady Pembroke asked, turning to her brother.

He stepped closer, studying the effect. Eva caught the scent of sandalwood and clean linen as he leaned in.

"Miss Hartwell is correct," he said. "The colour suits you admirably."

When the fitting concluded and designs were selected, Eva began gathering the fabric samples. Lord Pembroke approached as his sister discussed final details with Miss Adelaide.

"You have quite the artistic eye, Miss Hartwell," he said quietly. "Your suggestions are ... inspired."

Eva looked up, surprised by the genuine admiration in his voice. "Thank you, my lord. I merely thought the butterflies along the embroidery would complement Lady Pembroke's lively nature."

"You discerned that in such a brief acquaintance?" His eyes crinkled with amusement. "Impressive."

"A seamstress must be observant," Eva replied, a small smile playing at her lips.

"Indeed." He studied her face for a moment longer than propriety might allow. "I look forward to seeing the finished creation."

As the Pembrokes departed, Eva returned to her workstation, her heart beating a peculiar rhythm. She caught Miss Adelaide watching her with a knowing expression.

"Lord Pembroke seemed quite taken with your suggestions," Miss Adelaide remarked casually.

Eva bent her head over her work, hoping to hide the flush in her cheeks. "He was merely being polite."

"Perhaps," Miss Adelaide replied, though her tone suggested otherwise. "In any case, Lady Pembroke's gown will be our priority. It seems we'll be attending Lady Harrington's garden party after all."

Eva nodded, her fingers resuming their dance across fabric and thread, but her mind remained filled with deep blue eyes and the unexpected warmth of genuine appreciation.

THE GARDEN PARTY

*T*he Harrington estate sprawled before them in pristine splendour, its manicured gardens an explosion of summer blooms. Eva tugged at the sleeve of her blue dress, still unused to wearing something so fine instead of making such garments for others.

"Stop fidgeting," Miss Adelaide whispered as their carriage approached the grand entrance. "Remember, we're here as invited guests, not servants."

Eva nodded, straightening her shoulders. "It's just—I've never attended anything so grand."

"Nor had I, until my first society event. Simply observe, speak when spoken to, and remember that your work adorns half the ladies present."

The footman helped them descend from the carriage. Eva's eyes widened at the spectacle before her—elegant women in pastel silks floated across the lawn like exotic butterflies, while gentlemen in crisp summer attire gathered in clusters beneath white pavilions.

Miss Adelaide smiled. "I see Mrs Worthington wearing your design—the pale green with rosettes along the bodice."

Eva spotted the woman immediately, her heart swelling with pride. "And there's Mrs Fenwick in the blue day dress we finished last week."

"Indeed. Our handiwork is everywhere."

They made their way through the crowd, Miss Adelaide nodding graciously to various acquaintances. Eva felt the weight of curious glances, some appreciative, others dismissive once they noted her simple attire.

"Miss Thornton!" Mrs Harrington approached, resplendent in a cream gown with gold embroidery—one of Eva's earliest designs at the shop. "How delightful you could attend. And this must be your prodigy I've heard whispers about."

"Mrs Harrington, may I present Miss Evangeline Hartwell, whose artistic vision has contributed significantly to our recent designs."

Eva curtseyed. "An honour, ma'am. Your home is beautiful."

"Such lovely manners, though I detect an accent. American, is it not?"

"Yes, ma'am. From Boston originally."

Mrs Harrington's eyebrows rose with interest. "How fascinating! Thomas, come meet this charming American girl. She designed half the gowns here today!"

Soon Eva found herself surrounded by curious ladies, each eager to discover how an American had mastered European fashion sensibilities. Their questions came in rapid succession:

"Is it true American women prefer bold colours?"

"Do Boston ladies follow Paris fashions or create their own?"

"What brought you across the Atlantic?"

Eva answered each query with growing confidence, careful to mention only her Boston upbringing and father's naval career, avoiding any hint of workhouses or hardship.

"I find English sensibilities suit me perfectly," she explained when asked if she missed American styles. "There's an elegance here that feels like home now."

"You've certainly captured that elegance in my daughter's gown," an elderly duchess remarked. "She's received countless compliments today."

Miss Adelaide beamed beside her, occasionally steering the conversation when questions veered toward Eva's family background.

They had just broken free from the crowd when a familiar voice called out.

"Miss Thornton! Miss Hartwell!"

Lady Scarlett Pembroke approached, resplendent in the lavender silk gown Eva had designed, butterflies embroidered along the hem seeming to take flight with each step.

"You've created absolute magic," Scarlett said, taking Eva's hands in hers. "Everyone has been asking about this gown."

"It suits you perfectly, my lady," Eva replied, genuinely pleased at how the design had come to life.

"Please, when we're away from stuffy formalities, call me Scarlett." She turned to include Miss Adelaide in her warm smile. "Both of you must come meet my friends. I've been telling them about your remarkable shop."

With gentle insistence, Scarlett led them through the crowd toward a small gathering beneath a flowering cherry tree. Eva felt a flutter in her chest when she recognised Lord Pembroke among them.

He turned as they approached, his conversation falling silent mid-sentence. His eyes found Eva's immediately.

"Miss Thornton, Miss Hartwell," he greeted them with a slight bow. "I see my sister has claimed you as her newest treasures."

Scarlett laughed. "Don't be ridiculous, James. I'm merely introducing the creative minds behind half the fashion at this gathering."

The next half-hour passed in a pleasant blur as Eva met various members of London's elite. Throughout the conversations, she noticed Lord Pembroke watching her with quiet interest, particularly when she spoke of design inspirations or responded to questions about America.

When the small orchestra began playing a waltz, the group dispersed toward the dance floor. Miss Adelaide was drawn into conversation with a fabric merchant, leaving Eva momentarily alone with Lord Pembroke.

"Your creation has transformed my sister," he said, nodding toward Scarlett, who twirled among the dancers. "I've never seen her receive so many compliments."

"The dress merely complements what was already there," Eva replied.

"Modesty as well as talent." His smile reached his eyes, creating small crinkles at the corners. "Tell me, Miss Hartwell, do you dance as skilfully as you sew?"

Eva glanced toward the dancers. "I fear not, my lord. My education in such matters was ... interrupted by circumstance."

Understanding flickered across his face. "Perhaps another time, then. And please, when we're conversing like this, I'd prefer if you called me James."

"I couldn't possibly—"

"You could," he insisted gently. "Formality often stands in the way of genuine conversation, don't you think?"

The warmth in his eyes made her breath catch. "As you wish ... James."

His name felt strange yet right on her tongue, like tasting exotic fruit for the first time.

"There," he said with satisfaction. "Much better."

Their moment was interrupted by Scarlett's return, flushed from dancing. "James, you're monopolising our guests! Come, Eva, you must try these marvellous little cakes."

The remainder of the afternoon passed in pleasant conversation and gentle laughter. By the time the sun began its descent, Eva's cheeks ached from smiling.

As their carriage pulled away from the Harrington estate, Miss Adelaide gave Eva's hand a squeeze. "You were magnificent today. They adored you."

"It was the dresses they admired, not me," Eva demurred, though she couldn't suppress her smile.

"Nonsense. And I noticed Lord Pembroke seemed particularly attentive."

Eva felt heat rise to her cheeks. "He was merely being polite."

"Was he indeed?" Miss Adelaide's eyes twinkled knowingly. "I've seen that young man at dozens of society events, Eva. He is unfailingly polite to everyone, yes, but rarely does he appear genuinely interested. Until today."

Eva gazed out the window, unable to contain the happiness bubbling within her. The setting sun gilded London's buildings, making even the humblest structures appear magnificent and full of possibility.

Eva felt herself looking forward rather than back—toward a future bright with promise and perhaps something more, something she dared not name even in the privacy of her thoughts.

UNCERTAIN WATERS

The morning after the garden party, Eva's fingers moved deftly through the layers of silk and lace. Her mind wandered back to Lord Pembroke's—James'—smile, the warmth in his eyes when he'd asked her to use his given name. She caught herself smiling and quickly composed her features, focusing on the intricate beadwork before her.

"Your needlework is particularly fine today," Miss Adelaide observed, startling Eva from her reverie. "Perhaps inspired by yesterday's success?"

Eva's cheeks warmed. "The Harrington party was educational," she replied diplomatically. "I've never seen so many fine garments in one place."

"Indeed." Miss Adelaide's knowing smile suggested she understood exactly what—or whom—had truly captured Eva's attention.

The bell above the shop door jingled, announcing a customer. Eva glanced up, needle poised mid-stitch, and nearly pricked her finger when Lord James Pembroke himself strode into the shop, removing his top hat with practiced elegance.

"Good morning, Miss Thornton, Miss Hartwell." His eyes lingered on Eva. "I hope I'm not interrupting."

"Not at all, Lord Pembroke," Miss Adelaide replied. "What brings you to our humble establishment today?"

"My sister was so pleased with her gown that she's commissioned several more pieces. She's sent me with her preferences." He produced a sealed envelope. "Though I confess, I volunteered for the errand."

Eva busied herself with her work, conscious of his gaze upon her.

"Would you care to see our latest designs while you're here?" Miss Adelaide suggested. "Perhaps Miss Hartwell could show you the sketches for autumn."

Eva looked up to find James already watching her, a slight curve to his lips. "I would be delighted."

By the following week, James had visited the shop three more times—once to confirm details of Scarlett's order, once to commission a waistcoat for himself — "Only Miss Hartwell's design will suffice," he'd insisted — and once bearing a donation of fine fabrics from his mother's collection for a charity project.

On his fourth visit, he arrived during a quiet afternoon lull. Eva was alone in the front of the shop, arranging a display.

"You've transformed this window," he commented, admiring her work. "The way you've draped that midnight blue velvet creates the perfect backdrop."

Eva turned, surprised by his artistic observation. "You have an eye for design, my lord."

"James," he corrected gently. "And perhaps I'm developing one through our conversations."

Eva smiled, feeling uncharacteristically bold. "Very well,

James. Though you risk scandalising Miss Thornton with such informality."

"I believe Miss Thornton is more progressive than most give her credit for." His eyes sparkled with mischief. "Besides, I've brought something that might earn her forgiveness."

From behind his back, James produced a book, bound in worn leather.

"Wordsworth's poems," Eva breathed, accepting the volume with reverent hands. "How did you know?"

"You mentioned your fondness for his descriptions of nature during our conversation at the garden party." He gestured to the book. "This edition belonged to my father. I thought you might enjoy it."

Eva carefully opened the cover, running her fingertips over the yellowed pages. "I couldn't possibly accept something so precious."

"It's merely on loan," he insisted. "I expect a full discussion of your favourite passages when next we meet."

Their next meeting came sooner than expected when James arrived the following day with an invitation for Miss Thornton's shop to display their work at a charity exhibition for orphaned children.

"The committee needs examples of quality workmanship," he explained to Miss Adelaide, though his eyes frequently strayed to Eva. "Your designs would certainly elevate the affair."

After discussing details with Miss Adelaide, James lingered by Eva's workstation. "Have you had a chance to read any Wordsworth?"

"Two poems last night," Eva confessed. "'I Wandered Lonely as a Cloud' reminded me of walks I took as a child with my father."

THE CAPTAIN'S LOST DAUGHTER

James leaned against her table, his voice softening. "You seldom speak of your family."

Eva's fingers stilled on her embroidery. "There's little to tell. My mother died when I was young. My father ..." Her throat tightened. "He was lost at sea."

James' hand moved as if to cover hers, then withdrew, mindful of propriety. "I'm truly sorry, Eva."

The gentle sincerity in his voice wrapped around her heart. In that moment, the distance between their stations seemed to vanish.

Miss Adelaide approached with tea, her arrival both a welcome interruption and gentle reminder of boundaries. Over steaming cups, their conversation flowed easily between literature, art, and James' charitable endeavours.

"You've given these children more than shelter," Eva observed when he described the orphanage his family supported. "You've given them dignity."

Something shifted in James' expression—recognition, perhaps, of the depth of understanding behind her words. "Not everyone sees it that way."

"Their blindness doesn't diminish your work's value," Eva replied firmly.

James studied her face. "How is it you understand so well what others cannot see?"

Eva's gaze dropped to her teacup. "Perhaps I've simply observed life from different vantage points than most."

As summer waned into autumn, James' visits became a regular occurrence. He brought books they discussed in quiet corners of the shop, interesting fabrics he'd encountered in his travels, and once, a small bouquet of wildflowers "that matched the colour of that dress you were designing."

With each visit, Eva felt herself drawn further into his world —a world of ideas, compassion, and possibilities she'd never dared imagine. Yet shadows of doubt lingered. During a quiet moment while they examined patterns together, their hands accidentally brushed. The jolt of awareness that passed between them made Eva step back.

"Is something wrong?" James asked.

"This ... friendship between us," Eva began carefully. "I fear it may cause difficulties for you."

Understanding dawned in his eyes. "You mean because of our different stations."

"A nobleman and a seamstress are not typical companions."

James' expression grew serious. "I've never much cared for typicality, Eva. When I look at you, I don't see a seamstress."

"What do you see?" she whispered.

"A woman of extraordinary courage and grace." His voice lowered. "Someone who makes me question everything I once took for granted."

The intensity in his gaze both thrilled and frightened her. Eva had survived by being practical, by understanding the harsh realities of the world. Whatever was growing between them existed in dangerous opposition to those realities.

"Your family would never approve," she murmured.

James' jaw tightened. "My family doesn't dictate my heart."

The word "heart" hung between them, neither willing to acknowledge its full implication.

"Eva," Miss Adelaide called from the front of the shop, "Lady Harrington has arrived for her fitting."

Eva stepped back, grateful for the interruption yet aching at the distance it created. "I must go."

James nodded, his eyes never leaving hers. "I'll return tomorrow."

It wasn't a question, and Eva didn't pretend it was. "I'll have finished reading the Byron book by then."

His smile returned. "I look forward to hearing your thoughts."

As Eva moved to attend Lady Harrington, she caught Miss Adelaide's concerned glance. Her mentor's eyes held both warning and compassion—the look of someone who understood precisely how treacherous the path ahead might be.

KINDLING FLAMES

The autumn breeze carried whispers of change through London's streets as Eva stood in Thornton's shop, arranging a display of new ribbons. The bell above the door jingled, and she turned to find James standing there, hat in hand, his expression warm.

"Good morning, Eva. I was hoping to find you here."

Eva smiled, tucking a loose strand of golden hair behind her ear. "Where else would I be? This is my place of work."

"Actually, I was wondering if you might consider a brief respite from your labours. The weather is uncommonly fine today."

"What did you have in mind?"

He produced a small wicker basket from behind his back. "I've taken the liberty of preparing a modest picnic. Hyde Park is particularly lovely this time of year. We could read ..." He pulled a book from his coat pocket. "I've brought Keats."

Eva glanced toward Miss Adelaide, who was pretending not to listen while adjusting a mannequin's sleeve.

"Go on," Miss Adelaide said without looking up. "The

autumn collection is well ahead of schedule, thanks to your diligence. A few hours of fresh air will do you good."

"Are you certain?"

"Quite certain." Miss Adelaide finally turned, her eyes twinkling. "Though I expect you back before closing."

Twenty minutes later, Eva found herself seated beside James on a blanket spread beneath a golden-leaved oak. The park buzzed with distant activity—children laughing, couples strolling, vendors calling their wares—but their spot remained pleasantly secluded.

"This is lovely," Eva said, taking in the tableau of autumn colours. "I rarely venture here, despite it being so close to the shop."

"All work and no leisure makes for a dull existence," James replied, opening the basket to reveal bread, cheese, apples, and a small jar of honey.

They took turns reading passages aloud from their favourite books. Eva shared tales of adventure from her childhood readings, while James recited poetry with such feeling that the words seemed to dance in the air between them.

"Listen to this," Eva said excitedly, reading from a novel. "'The sea calls to those with adventure in their blood. It promises nothing but offers everything to those brave enough to answer.'"

James watched her, captivated by the animation in her face. "You still miss it, don't you? The sea."

"Sometimes I dream I'm back on my father's ship, feeling the deck sway beneath my feet." Her voice softened. "But England has become home now, in ways I never expected."

"I'm glad of that," he said quietly, reaching into his pocket. "I found this yesterday and thought of you."

He handed her a small package wrapped in tissue paper. Inside lay a delicate hair ribbon in sapphire blue, embroidered with tiny silver stars.

"James, it's beautiful."

"It reminded me of the night sky over the ocean you described." His fingers brushed hers as she took it. "I thought perhaps you might incorporate something similar in your next design."

"You've quite the eye for detail."

"Only when it matters." His gaze held hers a moment too long.

These thoughtful gifts had become a pattern—a pressed flower that matched her skirt, a unique button he'd discovered in a market, a scrap of exotic fabric from his travels. Each one showed how closely he observed her, how he connected with her creative spirit.

As weeks passed, they fell into a rhythm of stolen moments. Sometimes they would stand by the shop window as sunset painted London in amber hues, watching people hurry home.

"Look at that gentleman," James would say. "Rushing to meet his sweetheart, I'd wager."

"No," Eva would counter, laughing. "Late for dinner with his mother-in-law. See how his shoulders are hunched?"

Their observations would dissolve into laughter that lingered in the air, creating invisible threads binding them together.

One evening, as twilight settled over the city, James' expression grew serious. "My sister asked about you today."

Eva's hands stilled on the fabric she was arranging. "Oh?"

"She thinks you're remarkable. She's quite taken with your designs." He hesitated. "But she also warned me that our family won't approve of my spending so much time with a seamstress."

"She's right," Eva said softly.

"She's wrong," James countered. "About what matters, at least."

Eva changed the subject, but his words lingered in her mind long after he'd gone.

THE CAPTAIN'S LOST DAUGHTER

The following week, James appeared at the shop door just before closing time, carrying a covered basket that emitted enticing aromas.

"I thought perhaps you and Miss Adelaide might enjoy something other than cold tea and biscuits for supper tonight," he announced.

Miss Adelaide looked up in surprise. "Lord Pembroke, you shouldn't have troubled yourself."

"It was no trouble. My cook prepared more than enough, and I thought ..." His eyes found Eva's. "Well, I thought it might be nice to share a meal together."

They gathered around the small table in the back room, the shop's sign turned to "Closed." James unveiled dishes of roasted chicken, vegetables, and freshly baked bread. The simplicity of sharing food transformed the workspace into something intimate and warm.

"This is wonderful," Eva said, watching James interact easily with Miss Adelaide, asking about her family in Sussex and listening attentively to her stories of establishing the shop.

When Miss Adelaide excused herself to fetch tea, James leaned slightly toward Eva.

"I've never seen you look more beautiful than you do right now," he said softly.

"I'm hardly at my best," she protested. "I've been working all day."

"That's precisely why," he replied. "You're animated, engaged. There's a fire in your eyes when you speak about things you care about. It's ... captivating."

Their hands lay inches apart on the table. Eva felt the air between them charged with unspoken feelings. When she reached for the salt, their fingers brushed, and the contact sent warmth flooding through her.

They both froze, eyes meeting in silent acknowledgment of the current that passed between them. Eva saw her own surprise mirrored in his expression, along with something deeper that made her heart race.

Miss Adelaide returned with the tea tray, breaking the moment, but the evening continued bathed in a new awareness that neither could deny. Something had shifted, something Eva had neither invited nor expected but could no longer ignore.

As James prepared to leave, he paused at the door, his eyes finding Eva's across the room.

"Until tomorrow?" he asked quietly.

Eva nodded, knowing that whatever path lay ahead, she had already begun to walk it.

SHARING STORIES

The clock chimed four in Miss Thornton's shop as Eva pinned a bodice to a dressmaker's dummy. Outside, rain pattered against the windows, transforming London's streets into shimmering mirrors. Few customers ventured out in such weather, leaving the shop unusually quiet.

When the bell above the door jingled, Eva knew without looking who had arrived. James shook raindrops from his coat and hat, his smile warming the room more effectively than the small coal fire in the corner.

"Lord Pembroke," Miss Adelaide greeted him. "What brings you out in such dreadful weather?"

"I was in the neighbourhood and thought I might seek shelter until the worst passes." His eyes found Eva's across the room. "Besides, I promised to return that book I borrowed from Miss Hartwell."

Miss Adelaide glanced between them, her expression knowing. "Well then, I shall leave you to your literary discussion. I have accounts to settle in the back room."

When they were alone, James crossed to Eva's workstation. "In truth, I had no errands nearby. I simply wished to see you."

Eva's cheeks warmed. "You'll catch your death in this rain."

"Worth every drop." He pulled a chair beside her table, watching as her fingers worked nimbly with pins and silk. "What are you creating today?"

"A commission for Mrs Lester's daughter. Her coming-out ball is next month."

Silence settled comfortably between them as Eva worked and James observed. Rain drummed steadily on the roof, cocooning them in a world of their own.

"I've been wondering something," Eva said finally, her curiosity overcoming her reserve. "About your title."

"What about it?"

"You and Lady Scarlett seem quite young to be—" She hesitated, wondering if she'd overstepped.

"To be Lord and Lady Pembroke?" James finished for her. He sighed, leaning back in his chair. "We inherited the titles earlier than expected. Our parents died in a carriage accident about three years ago."

Eva's hands stilled on the fabric. "I'm so sorry."

"It was raining, rather like today." His voice softened with memory. "The horses spooked at something on the road. The carriage overturned near Hampstead Heath. My father died instantly. Mother lingered for two days but never regained consciousness."

"That's terrible," Eva whispered.

"Suddenly Scarlett and I were thrust into roles we weren't prepared for. I was barely nineteen." He ran a hand through his damp hair. "My aunt and uncle—Agatha and Frederick—moved into the estate to help oversee things, but they can be rather ..."

"Overbearing?" Eva suggested gently.

James' smile returned. "Precisely. They mean well, I suppose. Uncle Frederick handles most of the business affairs, while Aunt Agatha concerns herself with our social standing. She's determined to see me married to someone suitable."

"I've heard rumours ..." Eva said lightly, remembering a beautiful woman who occasionally visited the shop.

"You have?" James looked slightly embarrassed.

"One Lady Catherine Darrington." Eva said. "She's very pretty."

"Aunt Agatha's choice, not mine." His eyes met Eva's. "But enough about that. What of your parents? You mentioned your father was lost at sea."

Eva set down her pins, the familiar ache rising in her chest. "My mother died of consumption when I was seven. Father couldn't bear to stay in Boston afterward—too many memories. He accepted a position with a shipping company in Liverpool." She traced the pattern on the silk with her fingertip. "We were one day from Liverpool when the storm hit."

"The SS Lydia," James said quietly.

Eva looked up, surprised. "How did you know?"

"I remember reading about it. A terrible tragedy."

"Father got me into a lifeboat, but went back to help others." Eva's voice remained steady, though the memory still cut deep. "The last I saw of him, he was on the deck as the ship went down. Our lifeboat capsized near the shore. I was the only one who made it to land."

James reached across the table, his warm hand covering hers. "To lose both parents, and in such ways. I can't imagine your courage, Eva."

"Not courage," she said. "Just survival."

"No. It's more than that." His fingers tightened around hers. "Anyone can merely survive. You've built something beautiful from the ashes."

They sat in silence, the rain creating a gentle backdrop to their shared grief. Eva felt a strange comfort in his presence—in knowing he understood what it meant to have your world torn apart, to rebuild something new from the remnants.

"Sometimes I still expect to see them," James admitted. "I'll hear a laugh that sounds like Mother's, or catch a glimpse of someone who moves like Father did. For a moment, I forget they're gone."

"I dream of my father walking through the door," Eva confessed. "In my dreams, he was never lost at sea—merely delayed. He comes to find me, and everything makes sense again."

"Does it get easier?" James asked.

"Different, not easier. The pain changes shape." Eva met his gaze. "But we carry on. What choice do we have?"

"None, I suppose." He smiled sadly. "Though it helps to find someone who understands."

"Yes," she agreed softly. "It does."

Outside, the rain began to lessen, and slivers of late afternoon sunlight broke through the clouds, casting patterns across the workroom floor. Neither moved to break the connection between their hands.

"My aunt believes grief should be properly managed," James said. "Contained within appropriate mourning periods, expressed in socially acceptable ways. She found my behaviour quite unseemly when I disappeared for days after the funeral."

"Where did you go?"

"To our summer cottage by the sea. I needed to hear the waves, to feel small against something vast and unchanging." He paused. "I suspect you understand that better than most."

"The sea both terrifies and comforts me," Eva admitted. "It took my father, yet somehow I feel closest to him when I stand at the shore."

James nodded. "That's how I feel about riding across our estate. Father taught me every inch of that land. When I'm there, it's almost as if—"

"—they're still with you," Eva finished.

Their eyes met in perfect understanding, a bridge forming between their separate islands of loss. In that moment, Eva recognised something profound: beneath the differences in their stations lay a shared landscape of grief and resilience that made them more alike than different.

"I should go," James said finally, though he made no move to leave. "The rain has stopped."

"Yes," Eva agreed, equally reluctant to break the spell between them.

When he finally rose to leave, he hesitated by her table. "Thank you, Eva. For sharing your story. For listening to mine."

"Thank you for understanding," she replied simply.

As the shop door closed behind him, Eva realised that something fundamental had shifted between them—a deeper connection forged in the quiet acknowledgment of shared pain and the tentative hope that perhaps neither needed to walk their path alone.

TURNING TIDES

Marcus Billington swirled amber brandy in his crystal tumbler, observing the evening streets from his office window. The gaslight cast long shadows across cobblestones, illuminating a familiar figure emerging from Thornton's Fine Dressmaking & Alterations. Lord James Pembroke lingered at the shop door, casting one last glance inside before striding away with uncharacteristic lightness in his step.

"Fourth visit this week," Billington murmured, lips curling into a calculating smile.

He stepped back from the window, retreating into the opulent dimness of his private sanctuary. Mahogany panelling and leather-bound books created an atmosphere of refined wealth, a testament to his rise from obscurity to power. Yet it wasn't enough. It would never be enough.

Billington placed his untouched drink on his desk and ran a finger along a shipping ledger. The Pembroke family name glared up at him from the pages—their shipyard contracts, their exclusive importing rights, their stranglehold on the most profitable routes to India and the Americas. All of it should have been his.

"Love makes men weak," he said to the empty room, "and weakness can be exploited."

The young lord's infatuation with the seamstress had not escaped Billington's notice. His network of informants—shopkeepers, clerks, and servants strategically placed throughout London—reported Pembroke's movements with clockwork precision. The aristocrat's interest in a common girl was precisely the sort of vulnerability Billington had been waiting for.

He unlocked a hidden drawer in his desk and withdrew a thick portfolio of documents. Meticulously organised papers detailed his systematic dismantling of the Pembroke shipping enterprise: captains bribed to delay critical shipments, customs officials paid to "misplace" cargo manifests, competing merchants incentivised to undercut Pembroke contracts.

"Three years of groundwork," Billington muttered, reviewing his handiwork. "And now the final piece reveals itself."

He'd nearly bankrupted the Pembrokes through a thousand small cuts. Their ships still sailed, their name remained respected, but their finances teetered on a precipice few suspected. One significant blow would send them tumbling into ruin, and their docklands properties—prime real estate Billington coveted—would be his for a fraction of their worth.

A knock at the door interrupted his thoughts.

"Enter," Billington commanded, quickly returning the portfolio to its hiding place.

The door creaked open to reveal a stooped figure. Archibald Mountforth's balding head caught the lamplight as he shuffled in, hat clutched in his hands. Despite his obsequious posture, cruelty glinted in his grey eyes.

"You're late, Mountforth."

"Forgive me, Mr Billington. The evening workhouse inspection couldn't be rushed." Mountforth bowed slightly. "The new shipment of children from the country parishes required ... processing."

Billington gestured to a chair. "Sit. I've something more profitable to discuss than your workhouse operations."

Mountforth perched on the edge of the chair, his heavy jowls quivering with anticipation. "You mentioned a special arrangement in your message, sir?"

"Indeed." Billington poured a second glass of brandy and pushed it across the desk. "Tell me, how many inmates have escaped your care over the years?"

Mountforth's face darkened. "Ungrateful wretches, the lot of them. Perhaps a couple dozen have managed it. That fire at Middleford two years ago cost me sixteen alone."

"And legally, these escapees remain under your jurisdiction?"

"Naturally. Parish law is quite clear. Once assigned to a workhouse, they're bound until properly discharged." Mountforth took a greedy sip of brandy. "Or dead."

Billington's smile didn't reach his eyes. "What would you say to an arrangement whereby these escapees are returned to you—for a suitable fee, of course—and then contracted out to my factories at special rates?"

Mountforth's small eyes widened. "You know where some of my runaways are?"

"I know where one is. A girl. She'll serve as our test case." Billington leaned forward. "She appears to have made something of herself. All the more satisfying to remind her of her proper place."

"And my compensation?"

"Ten pounds per recaptured inmate, plus a percentage of their contracted labour value." Billington watched greed overtake caution in Mountforth's expression. "You'll need to provide legal documentation, of course. Papers showing your authority to reclaim them."

"Child's play," Mountforth waved dismissively. "I've the proper forms in my office. A few signatures, the parish seal—all quite official."

"Excellent." Billington rose and moved to a cabinet, withdrawing a slim folder. "My man has been following one particular young woman. Approximately eighteen years old, golden hair, works as a seamstress at Thornton's shop on Bond Street." He slid a crude sketch across the desk. "Does she look familiar?"

Mountforth squinted at the image, then his face contorted with malicious recognition. "Well, well. If it isn't little Miss Evangeline Hartwell." He practically spat the name. "Oh yes, I remember her well. Thought herself above the rest. Organised that fire, I'm certain of it."

"Then you can identify her as your escaped inmate?"

"Without question. Been seeking her for nearly two years." Mountforth's fingers trembled with excitement. "When do we collect her?"

"Patience, Mountforth." Billington refilled their glasses. "This particular girl has powerful friends. Lord James Pembroke has taken a special interest in her."

"A lord?" Mountforth sneered. "What's a nobleman want with workhouse rubbish?"

"That's immaterial." Billington's voice hardened. "What matters is timing. I need to maximise the girl's value before reclaiming her."

Billington summoned his manservant with a bell pull. "Franklin, bring in Barrett."

Moments later, a thin man with rat-like features slipped into the room. His clothes were respectable but unremarkable—designed to blend into any crowd.

"Report," Billington commanded.

Barrett bowed slightly. "The girl keeps to a predictable

schedule, sir. Starts work at the shop by seven each morning. Works until seven in the evening. Shares lodgings above the shop with the proprietress."

"Friends? Connections?"

"Few beyond the shop. Occasionally visits a group of street children near Blackstock Road. Brings them food, mends their clothes." Barrett's thin lips twisted. "Playing the lady bountiful with her new station."

"And Pembroke's interest?"

"Increasingly obvious. Visits nearly daily, brings gifts. They've been seen walking in Hyde Park together. The shop owner appears to chaperone, but often leaves them alone."

Billington nodded thoughtfully. "Continue your surveillance. I want to know everyone she speaks to, everywhere she goes. Pay particular attention to her interactions with Pembroke."

After dismissing Barrett, Billington turned back to Mountforth. "Prepare your papers, but take no action until I give the word. The timing must be perfect."

When Mountforth had gone, Billington returned to his window. Night had fully descended on London now, the streets emptier save for the occasional carriage or desperate soul. In the distance, the Thames reflected the city's lights—a dark ribbon binding together the empire's heart.

Marcus Billington stood tall against the cityscape, a silhouette cut from ambition and malice. London lay spread before him like a feast, and he intended to devour his portion and more.

"The Pembrokes have sailed smooth waters for generations," he whispered to the glass. "It's time they learned how quickly the tide can turn."

DISTANT HOPE

Rain hammered against London's cobblestones, transforming neat streets into muddy rivers. Eva clutched her shawl tighter, struggling to keep her small bundle of flowers dry beneath its meager protection. The delicate blooms—pale roses and sprigs of lavender—had been arranged with care, their faint fragrance a sharp contrast to the damp, smoky air surrounding her.

Despite working at Thornton's, Eva still sold flowers occasionally. The extra coins meant another loaf for the children at Blackstock Road or a new ribbon for her workbox. More importantly, it kept her connected to the streets that had been her first London home.

"Fresh flowers! Brighten your day with fresh flowers!" Her voice barely carried above the downpour and the clattering of carriage wheels.

Two pennies jingled in her pocket—hardly enough for an evening meal. Eva sighed, brushing a damp golden curl from her forehead. Miss Adelaide had given her the afternoon off, a rare luxury Eva had intended to use visiting her friends near Blackstock Road. The sudden storm had other plans.

She paused beneath the awning of a fruit seller, watching people scurry past. Despite the weather, Covent Garden market pulsed with life—merchants haggling, women gossiping over baskets of vegetables, children darting between stalls.

"Mark my words, another ship gone down off Portsmouth," a gruff voice declared nearby. "Third this month."

"It's them new steam vessels," his companion replied. "Dangerous business, pushing against nature that way."

Eva's attention drifted to their conversation, the familiar pang of loss surfacing at any mention of maritime disaster. Though years had passed since the SS Lydia sank, such news always transported her back to that terrible night—the howling wind, her father's face disappearing beneath the waves.

She moved along, carefully stepping around a particularly deep puddle. The rain showed no signs of abating. Perhaps she should abandon her selling efforts and seek shelter in a tearoom until it passed.

As Eva considered her options, her gaze fell upon a man standing beneath the awning of The Crossed Anchors tavern. Something about his weathered stance caught her attention—the way he held himself, perhaps, or the careful manner in which his eyes scanned the crowd.

He wore a sailor's coat, its blue fabric faded by sun and salt. His beard was neatly trimmed, but his face bore the deep lines of one who had spent decades staring into horizon winds. There was something hauntingly familiar about him that Eva couldn't place.

The sailor's gaze swept across the market and suddenly locked with Eva's. His eyes widened slightly. He straightened, peering more intently through the rainfall, then stepped forward into the downpour without hesitation.

Eva clutched her flowers tighter as he approached, uncertain whether to retreat or stand her ground.

"Pardon me, miss," he said, removing his cap. Water dripped

from its brim as he twisted it in calloused hands. "Might seem strange, but you look familiar. Your face ..."

"I don't believe we've met, sir." Eva's response was polite but guarded.

"The name's Jameson. I sailed on the SS Amity, and before that ..." He paused, studying her features more carefully. "Good heavens. You're one of the Hartwell's!"

Eva's breath caught. Her fingers tightened around the flower stems until one snapped.

"How do you know that name?" Her voice emerged barely above a whisper.

"I'd know those eyes anywhere—same as the Captain's. You're his daughter, aren't you? The little girl from Boston." Jameson's expression softened with recognition. "We crossed paths years ago. I served under Captain Hartwell aboard the HMS Defiant before he left the navy."

The marketplace seemed to fade around Eva, the clamour of voices and rain receding into distant echoes. She reached for the brick wall beside her, steadying herself.

"My father ... You knew my father?"

"Aye, one of the finest officers I ever served under." Jameson nodded solemnly. "Word reached us about the SS Lydia going down. Terrible business."

Eva searched his face, afraid to voice the question burning within her. Finally, she gathered her courage.

"My father, Captain Thomas Hartwell. Did he—" The words caught in her throat. "Is there any chance he survived?"

Jameson's expression grew grave. "There was a terrible storm that night. The SS Lydia broke apart like kindling." He shook his head slowly, recalling the horror. "But aye, there were survivors."

Eva's heart hammered against her ribs. "My father? Do you know if—"

"Captain Hartwell was among them."

The flowers fell from Eva's fingers, scattering across the wet cobblestones. Her legs threatened to give way beneath her.

"He's alive?" The words came out as a desperate whisper, as if speaking too loudly might shatter this fragile hope.

"Last I heard." Jameson nodded, guiding Eva to a sheltered doorway as her balance faltered. "I wasn't there myself, you understand. But I heard the tale from Jenkins, who was rescued by the merchant vessel that responded to the wreckage."

"Where is he? My father?" Eva clutched Jameson's sleeve, heedless of propriety. "Please, I must know."

"When they pulled him from the water, he was badly injured. Blow to the head, they said. They took the survivors to Liverpool Royal Infirmary." Jameson's expression turned sympathetic. "The thing is, miss, Jenkins said your father couldn't remember much. Not even his own name at first."

"Memory loss?" Eva pressed her hand to her mouth.

"Aye. They identified him by papers in his coat and that brass compass he always wore." Jameson tapped his chest where such an item might hang. "Jenkins visited him twice before shipping out again. Said the Captain was recovering his strength but still confused about many things. That was nearly ten years ago now."

Eva's mind raced. Her father—alive but lost in his own memories. For years, she had mourned him, believing him dead while he lay in a hospital, perhaps wondering about the daughter he couldn't remember.

"I must go to him." The words tumbled out with fierce determination. "If he's in Liverpool, I need to—"

"Last Jenkins knew, he was still there," Jameson confirmed. "The doctors weren't sure if his memory would ever fully return, but physically he was mending well. Said something about him working with the hospital staff once he could walk again—helping with records or some such. Couldn't keep a good man idle, I suppose."

Tears welled in Eva's eyes, spilling down her cheeks to mingle with the raindrops. After so many years of loneliness and struggle, the possibility that her father still lived overwhelmed her.

"Thank you," she whispered, her voice thick with emotion. "You cannot know what this means to me."

"You have his eyes, you know." Jameson smiled kindly. "Same colour as the sea on a clear day. I'd know them anywhere."

KIDNAPPED

*E*va's fingers trembled as she threaded her needle the next morning. Her mind swirled with possibilities, hardly able to focus on the delicate embroidery before her. Father is alive. The thought repeated like a prayer, a mantra that buoyed her spirit despite the weight of ten years' separation.

"You seem distracted today," Miss Adelaide observed, placing a gentle hand on Eva's shoulder. "Is everything all right?"

"I must get to Liverpool," Eva blurted out, unable to contain the news any longer. "My father—he might be alive. A sailor recognised me yesterday. He said survivors from the SS Lydia were taken to Liverpool Royal Infirmary, and Father was among them."

Miss Adelaide's eyes widened. "Evangeline, that's extraordinary news! After all this time ..."

"He suffered memory loss from his injuries. That's why he never came looking for me." Eva's voice cracked. "I've been alone all these years while he was alive, not knowing who he was or that I existed."

"We'll find a way to get you there," Miss Adelaide promised, squeezing Eva's hand. "Perhaps after Lady Winterton's commission is complete next week—"

The shop bell jangled merrily, and a group of ladies swept in, bringing laughter and chatter that filled the small space. Eva tucked away her personal concerns and affixed a professional smile, moving to assist a young woman selecting ribbons for her bonnet.

The morning passed in a flurry of activity. Eva's hands worked steadily, but her thoughts drifted repeatedly to Liverpool and what might await her there. By midday, the shop buzzed with customers admiring the latest designs. Eva laughed as she demonstrated a new French pleating technique to an eager apprentice.

The bell above the door chimed again. Eva glanced up, her laugh dying in her throat.

Mr Mountforth stood in the doorway, his familiar scowl sending ice through her veins. Beside him loomed a well-dressed gentleman with cold, calculating eyes. The stranger stepped forward, his polished boots clicking against the wooden floor.

"Miss Hartwell!" he announced, his voice cutting through the shop's chatter. Several customers turned in curiosity. "I am Marcus Billington, representing the parish authorities."

Eva froze, the fabric slipping from her fingers.

"I have here," Billington continued, producing official-looking documents from his coat, "legal authorisation to reclaim a fugitive workhouse inmate who has been evading proper placement for over two years."

"There must be some mistake," Eva managed, her voice barely audible.

Mountforth's face twisted into a smirk. "No mistake, girl. You're property of Middleford Workhouse, and you've been stealing from the parish by running away."

"I am not—"

"Silence!" Mountforth snapped, stepping forward menacingly. "Your thieving ways end today."

Miss Adelaide pushed through the stunned customers. "What is the meaning of this? Miss Hartwell is my employee and a respected member of this establishment."

Billington offered a thin smile. "I'm afraid you've been deceived, madam. This girl is a documented ward of the parish, placed in Middleford Workhouse after washing ashore as an orphan. These papers clearly state—"

"I am not an orphan!" Eva protested, finding her voice. "My father is alive in Liverpool—"

"More lies," Mountforth scoffed. "Always were full of stories, weren't you? Captain's daughter indeed!"

Billington held up a hand. "The law is quite clear. Collect her, Mountforth."

Eva backed away as Mountforth advanced, bumping into a display of ribbons that cascaded to the floor. Ladies shrieked and scattered, some fleeing the shop entirely while others pressed against the walls, watching the drama unfold with horrified fascination.

"You have no right!" Miss Adelaide moved to stand between them. "I demand to see those papers properly!"

Billington coldly thrust the documents at Miss Adelaide. "Everything is in order. Interfere with an officer of the parish, and you risk your own establishment, madam."

Miss Adelaide scanned the papers, her face paling. Though Eva couldn't see the documents, she recognised the official stamps and signatures—fabricated or not, they carried weight.

"This is monstrous," Miss Adelaide whispered.

Mountforth seized Eva's arm with bruising force. "Come along, girl. You've had your little adventure."

"No!" Eva struggled, panic rising in her chest. "Miss Adelaide, please! They're lying!"

Customers scattered as Mountforth dragged Eva toward the

door, creating a chaotic scene of overturned displays and frightened gasps. Eva's heel caught on a fallen bolt of fabric, and she stumbled, nearly falling before Mountforth yanked her upright.

The shop door flew open just as they reached it. James Pembroke stood in the threshold, a bouquet of fresh spring blossoms in his hand. His expression shifted from anticipation to alarm as he took in the scene before him.

"What is happening here?" he demanded, his voice sharp with authority.

"Lord Pembroke," Billington said smoothly, a flash of something—recognition, calculation—crossing his features. "A parish matter. This young woman is being returned to her proper place."

"James!" Eva cried out, still struggling against Mountforth's grip. "They're lying! Please help me!"

James strode forward, but several fleeing customers blocked his path, creating a barrier of rustling skirts and flailing arms. "Release her at once!" he ordered, trying to push through the crush.

"The law is clear, my lord," Billington replied, his tone almost gloating. "We have full authority."

Mountforth dragged Eva through the doorway and down the steps to where a dark carriage waited at the curb. Eva caught a final glimpse of James' face—horror and determination etched across his features—before Mountforth roughly shoved her inside.

"James!" she screamed, lunging for the door as it slammed shut.

The carriage lurched forward with a crack of the whip. Through the small window, Eva saw James finally break free from the shop, sprinting into the street with desperate urgency. Their eyes met for one heart breaking moment before the carriage rounded a corner, and he disappeared from view.

Behind her, Billington's satisfied laugh filled the carriage's confined space. "Well done, Mountforth. Lord Pembroke's reaction was everything I hoped for."

Eva pressed herself against the far corner of the seat, her mind racing with terror and confusion. "What do you want with me?"

"You, my dear," Billington said, leaning forward with a predatory smile, "are merely a means to an end. The real prize is the look on young Pembroke's face when he realises exactly what he must sacrifice to get you back."

CAPTIVITY

The carriage wheels clattered over London's cobblestones as Eva pressed herself against the seat, heart hammering against her ribs. Billington sat opposite, watching her with the calculated interest of a collector examining a valuable acquisition.

"Where are you taking me?" Eva demanded, struggling to keep her voice steady.

"Somewhere your fine Lord Pembroke won't find you until I'm ready," Billington replied, straightening his already immaculate cuffs. "Though I must say, I'm rather impressed. A workhouse girl capturing the attention of one of England's most eligible bachelors—you've quite a talent for rising above your station."

Eva's mind raced through possible escapes. The carriage windows were small, the door securely latched. Mountforth's hulking presence beside Billington made any physical resistance futile.

"You know nothing about me," she said.

"On the contrary," Billington smiled thinly. "I know everything about you, Evangeline Hartwell. Orphaned in a shipwreck, taken in briefly by a fishwife, then properly placed in Middleford Workhouse where you belonged. Until you orchestrated that convenient fire, of course."

The carriage slowed, turning into a narrow lane flanked by towering brick buildings. Through the window, Eva glimpsed a forest of chimneys belching black smoke into the grey sky.

"My factory," Billington announced with proprietorial pride as the carriage halted. "One of many establishments where I create prosperity for England. Though some might find the conditions ... lacking in certain comforts."

Mountforth yanked open the door and dragged Eva onto the grimy cobblestones. Before her loomed a massive brick structure, its windows glazed with soot, the air around it thick with acrid smoke and the distant clanging of machinery.

Eva's breath caught in her throat. After escaping the workhouse, she'd sworn never to be imprisoned again. Yet here she stood, facing something perhaps even worse.

Billington led the way through an iron-studded door into a cavernous main floor. The noise hit Eva like a physical blow—the relentless pounding of machinery, the hiss of steam, the clatter of looms. Dozens of hollow-eyed workers, many no more than children, hunched over their stations, hands moving mechanically while overseers patrolled the aisles with leather straps hanging from their belts.

"Magnificent, isn't it?" Billington shouted over the din. "The engine of progress!"

Eva said nothing, her gaze fixed on a small boy, perhaps seven years old, who stumbled as he carried a heavy bobbin. An overseer's strap cracked across his shoulders, sending him sprawling.

"Don't waste your sympathy," Billington said, noting her expression. "Most would starve without my generosity."

They climbed a narrow staircase to the upper floor, where the noise diminished slightly. Billington unlocked a door revealing a room filled with a dozen workstations—sewing machines, cutting tables, and benches crowded together beneath grimy windows that allowed little light to penetrate.

"Your new domain," he announced, gesturing Eva inside. Several women and girls looked up briefly before returning to their work, their expressions carefully blank. "I believe you'll find the work familiar, if somewhat less ... refined than your recent employment."

Eva stepped into the room, feeling the walls closing in around her. "What do you want from me?"

Billington's smile widened. "Direct. I admire that." He closed the door behind them, leaving Mountforth standing guard outside. "It's quite simple. Lord Pembroke will receive a message tonight informing him of your situation. I'm offering a straightforward exchange—you for his family's shipping business and dock properties."

The breath left Eva's lungs. "He would never—"

"Oh, I think he might," Billington interrupted smoothly. "Young men in love make foolish decisions. Particularly when presented with evidence of their beloved's suffering." He ran a finger along a nearby sewing machine. "These can be dangerous devices when operated carelessly. Fingers caught, hands mangled ... tragic accidents happen daily in such establishments."

Eva's blood turned to ice. "You're despicable."

"I'm a businessman," Billington corrected. "The Pembrokes have something I want. You are merely the leverage I require to obtain it." He moved toward the door. "You'll work here like everyone else. Disobedience will be punished. Attempt to escape, and others will suffer for it."

He paused at the threshold. "I'll return you to him when the papers are signed—that's my promise. Whether you return intact depends entirely on your cooperation."

The door slammed shut behind him. Eva heard the key turn in the lock, sealing her fate.

For a moment, she stood frozen, the magnitude of her situation crashing over her like a tidal wave. Then a small voice broke the silence.

"You're the new one, then?" A thin girl of perhaps fourteen approached, her fingers raw and calloused. "I'm Mary."

Eva swallowed hard. "Eva."

"Best get to work before Simmons comes," Mary whispered, nodding toward a burly man visible through the window in the door. "He's quick with the strap."

Eva followed Mary to an empty station where a mountain of coarse fabric awaited hemming. The machine was ancient, its needle dulled from overuse. As she sat, Eva's gaze swept across the room, taking in the dozen pale faces bent over their work.

"How long have you been here?" Eva asked quietly.

Mary shrugged. "Two years, maybe? Days blur together. Some been here longer."

An older woman across the table glanced up. "Shut it, Mary. New ones always think they can change things. Can't."

The oppressive weight of hopelessness hung in the air, as tangible as the dust motes floating in the meagre shafts of light. Eva's fingers trembled as she threaded the machine, memories of the workhouse flooding back—the endless labour, the hunger, the beatings.

But alongside those memories came others: her father's laugh as he taught her to read the stars; her mother's gentle hands guiding her own through her first stitches; Miss Adelaide's kind smile; James' eyes, warm with admiration and something deeper.

Eva straightened her back. She might be imprisoned, but her spirit remained her own. Mountforth had underestimated her once—in thinking she would break. He would not make that mistake again.

As the machine rattled beneath her hands, Eva began to study the room, the windows, the guards' patterns. She would find a way out, not just for herself, but for all of them.

DIVIDED HEART

*J*ames paced before the ornate mahogany desk in his father's—no, his study now. The polished surface reflected lamplight in mocking brightness against the darkness consuming his thoughts. His hand trembled as he reached for Billington's letter again, though he'd memorised every vile word.

Lord Pembroke, I have something that belongs to you. Or perhaps I should say, someone you value beyond reason.

James hurled his empty tumbler into the fireplace. The crystal shattered with a satisfying crash, glass fragments catching the firelight before disappearing into the hearth.

"That won't bring her back."

He turned to find Scarlett standing in the doorway, her amber eyes filled with concern. She wore her riding habit, mud still clinging to the hem.

"I've been asking questions," she continued, closing the door softly behind her. "Discreetly, of course. Billington owns several factories across London. The worst of them is in Whitechapel—a textile mill where conditions are said to be ... barbaric."

James swallowed hard. "You think that's where he's keeping her?"

"It's likely." Scarlett crossed to stand beside him at the fireplace. "My lady's maid has a cousin who works for the Millers. She overheard Lord Miller discussing a scandal brewing—something about Billington using illegal workers, people forcibly taken from workhouses."

"Oh, Eva ..." James pressed his fist against the mantelpiece, struggling to breathe past the tightness in his chest. "This is my fault. If I hadn't been so obvious in my attentions—"

"Stop that immediately," Scarlett interrupted. "Billington has wanted our shipping business for years. He's merely found a vulnerability to exploit."

James turned to face his sister, struck by the fierce determination in her expression. "When did you become so formidable?"

A sad smile crossed her face. "When we were forced to become Lord and Lady Pembroke far too young, I suppose."

They fell silent, both gazing at their parents' portrait above the fireplace. The late Lord and Lady Pembroke stared back with painted eyes that couldn't offer the guidance James so desperately needed.

"I wish they were here," Scarlett whispered.

"Every day," James agreed. "Father would know how to handle Billington without capitulating."

"And Mother would have adored Eva." Scarlett squeezed his arm. "She always said character mattered more than circumstances."

The study door swung open without warning. Aunt Agatha swept in, her imposing figure draped in black silk that rustled with disapproval. Uncle Frederick followed, his face set in grave lines that deepened when he spotted the scattered glass by the hearth.

"Destruction of family heirlooms is hardly the behaviour of a man who claims to be protecting his legacy," Aunt Agatha observed coldly.

Scarlett straightened her spine. "Aunt, we were having a private—"

"This concerns the entire family, Scarlett," Uncle Frederick cut in. "The servants are whispering about a kidnapped seamstress. Is this true, James? Has Billington actually taken this ... person?"

James' jaw tightened. "Her name is Evangeline Hartwell."

"Her name is immaterial," Aunt Agatha snapped. "What matters is that you appear to be considering sacrificing generations of Pembroke prosperity over a common shop girl."

"She is not common," James replied, his voice dangerously quiet. "And yes, Billington has taken her. He's demanding our shipping company and the eastern docklands in exchange for her safety."

Uncle Frederick paled. "Preposterous! Those holdings represent half our family's worth!"

"Which is precisely why you cannot even contemplate such an exchange," Aunt Agatha declared, moving to stand directly before James. "I understand you've developed some ... affection for this girl. Young men often mistake infatuation for love. But you have responsibilities, James—to your family name, to your ancestors, to your future."

"To Lady Catherine," Uncle Frederick added pointedly. "The Darrington alliance would secure our position for generations. Her father has already agreed to the substantial dowry we discussed."

James felt his chest constrict. "You discussed a dowry without my knowledge?"

"Because you've been too distracted by your dalliance with a seamstress!" Aunt Agatha's voice rose. "Your parents did not die for you to squander their legacy on romantic notions. They expected you to lead this family with honour and prudence."

"Don't you dare invoke my parents in this," James growled. "You have no idea what they would have wanted."

"They would have wanted you to put family first," Uncle Frederick said flatly. "One seamstress is not worth the Pembroke name."

"The girl can be replaced," Aunt Agatha added with brutal pragmatism. "The docklands cannot."

Scarlett gasped. "How can you be so heartless? Eva is a person, not an object to be discarded!"

"Enough!" James' voice cut through the room like a whip crack. "Eva is being held captive because of me. Her life is in danger. I will not abandon her to Billington's cruelty."

Aunt Agatha's face hardened. "Then you abandon your duty instead. Your father would be ashamed."

The words struck like physical blows. James turned away, his hands gripping the edge of the desk until his knuckles whitened.

"The Darringtons are hosting their annual ball tomorrow evening," Uncle Frederick said after a tense silence. "Lady Catherine will expect your attendance. I suggest you use the occasion to secure your engagement and put an end to this unfortunate business."

"And what of Miss Hartwell?" Scarlett demanded.

"The authorities can be notified," Aunt Agatha replied dismissively. "Though I hardly think Billington would risk his reputation by actually harming the girl. This is merely a negotiation tactic."

James turned slowly, meeting his aunt's gaze with cold fury. "You think a man who kidnaps innocent women draws the line at hurting them?"

"I think," she replied evenly, "that you must decide whether you are the Lord Pembroke this family needs, or merely a lovesick boy playing at nobility."

She swept from the room, Uncle Frederick following after a

last troubled glance at his nephew. The door closed with a definitive click.

Scarlett moved to James' side. "You won't give in to them, will you?"

James stared at Billington's letter, at Eva's frightened eyes in the daguerreotype. "I don't know what to do, Scarlett," he admitted, his voice breaking. "If I defy the family to save Eva, I risk everything our parents built. If I abandon her to save our legacy..." He closed his eyes. "I don't know if I could live with myself."

The weight of responsibility pressed down upon him like a physical force. In that moment, James Pembroke felt the true burden of his title—torn between the woman who had awakened his heart and the duty that had defined his life.

BEYOND THESE WALLS

Eva's fingers ached as she wound bobbins in the dim factory light. Twelve hours into her captivity, her body protested the relentless work, but her mind remained untethered. She studied her surroundings methodically—the guards' rotation patterns, the locked doors, the tired faces of fellow prisoners.

Young Mary worked beside her, shoulders slumped in defeat. Eva leaned closer, keeping her voice low beneath the clatter of machinery.

"Have you ever seen the ocean, Mary?"

The girl startled at the unexpected question. "No, miss."

"I crossed an entire ocean once," Eva whispered, her hands never stopping their work. "Waves taller than this building crashed over our ship. I thought surely we'd perish, but we didn't—not all of us, anyway."

A few nearby workers glanced their way, hunger for something beyond their misery evident in their eyes.

"My father used to say that courage isn't the absence of fear, but moving forward despite it." Eva threaded a needle with practiced precision. "Like those waves—they seemed impossible to survive, yet here I stand."

Mary's hands trembled less as she resumed her work. "My mum said similar before the fever took her."

"Your mother was wise." Eva smiled softly. "What was her name?"

"Elizabeth," Mary answered, a flicker of life returning to her eyes.

By midday, Eva had learned five names, five stories. With each connection forged, spines straightened incrementally. When the factory bell signaled their meager lunch break, Eva moved among the children, teaching them to form a circle that shielded their whispered conversations from the guards.

"We'll sing while we work this afternoon," Eva suggested. "Something simple the overseers won't notice. When you feel afraid, remember you're not alone."

A tiny boy with hollow cheeks frowned. "What good's singing when we're locked in here?"

"It reminds us we're still human," Eva replied. "Billington can take our freedom for now, but he can't take what's inside us unless we surrender it."

That afternoon, a quiet hum rose from their workstations—barely audible beneath the machinery's roar, yet powerful in its defiance. The melody spread across the floor like a current, strengthening connections between strangers now united in resistance.

Night brought no reprieve. Eva lay on the hard wooden platform that served as a communal bed, her mind racing with half-formed escape plans. An elderly woman called Martha settled beside her, joints creaking with each movement.

"You've got spirit, girl," Martha murmured. "Reminds me of someone."

Eva turned toward her. "Who?"

"A sailor that delivers coal sometimes. Speaks of a Captain

who survived a terrible wreck years back. Lost his memories for the longest time, they say."

Eva's heart hammered against her ribs. "What captain?"

"Hartwell, I believe. Recovering at some hospital up north. Liverpool, maybe." Martha's weathered face creased with curiosity. "Means something to you, doesn't it?"

Eva clutched her chest where Mrs Fisher's brass button remained hidden in a small pocket she'd sewn into her undergarments. "That captain is my father."

"Well then," Martha whispered, "seems you've more reason than most to find your way out of here."

Eva stared into the darkness, fierce resolve crystallising within her. The news transformed her desperation into purpose. Her father had survived all these years—perhaps searching for her as she had mourned him. The thought blazed through her like wildfire.

"I will escape," Eva vowed under her breath. "Not just for myself or for James. I'll find my father and make us whole again."

She closed her eyes, mentally tracing the factory's layout, cataloguing potential allies, calculating risks. Sleep would not come tonight—not when freedom and family waited beyond these walls.

LOVE OR LEGACY

*J*ames sat at his father's desk, staring at the stack of documents Billington had delivered that morning. The thick parchment pages felt heavy in his hands —heavier than their physical weight suggested. Each clause, each legal term represented generations of Pembroke achievement, the legacy his father and grandfather before him had built through sweat and sacrifice.

And with a simple signature, he would give it all away.

He closed his eyes, and unbidden, Eva's face appeared in his mind. Her golden curls catching the afternoon light as they walked through Hyde Park. The slight furrow in her brow when she concentrated on a particularly complex embroidery. The way her eyes lit up when she spoke of the sea, transporting him to the vast blue expanse through her words alone.

"Billington you villain ..." he muttered, throwing the papers onto the desk.

James crossed to the window, gazing out at the London docks in the distance—Pembroke docks. Ships bearing the family crest sailed in and out daily, carrying cargo that sustained hundreds of families. The sailors, dockhands, clerks, and their dependents—all relied on the Pembroke name for their livelihoods.

Could he truly sacrifice them all for one woman?

But Eva wasn't just any woman. She had survived shipwreck, loss, and unspeakable hardship yet retained a compassion that humbled him. Her gentle strength had awakened something in him he hadn't known existed—a desire to be worthy of such goodness.

He poured himself a brandy, hardly tasting it as memories washed over him. Eva reading poetry aloud, her voice bringing Wordsworth's words to life in ways that made his heart ache with their beauty. The brush of her fingers against his when she'd accepted the blue ribbon with silver stars. Her laughter—God, her laughter—like music that resonated in chambers of his soul he'd never known existed.

The glass slipped from his hand, shattering on the hardwood floor.

"She's suffering right now," he whispered to the empty room.

James pictured Eva in that wretched factory, her delicate hands forced to work until they bled, surrounded by filth and cruelty. Because of him. Because Billington had recognised his weakness and exploited it mercilessly.

His family's voices echoed in his mind—Aunt Agatha's sharp disapproval, Uncle Frederick's pragmatic dismissal of Eva as "just a seamstress." Even Scarlett, though supportive, couldn't truly understand what Eva meant to him.

"A Pembroke marries for advantage, not sentiment," his aunt had lectured just yesterday. "Your father would be ashamed."

Would he, though? James remembered his father's quiet devotion to his mother—the way he'd looked at her across crowded ballrooms as if she were the only person present. Had that been mere duty?

He returned to the desk, picking up his pen. The nib hovered over the signature line as sweat beaded on his forehead.

If he signed, the Pembroke shipping empire would crumble. Generations of work undone by his hand. Hundreds left without employment. His family name tarnished forever.

If he refused, Eva would remain Billington's prisoner—or worse.

The pen trembled in his grasp.

Was there truly a choice? Could he live with himself if he abandoned her to save his fortune? What value would those ships and warehouses hold if he knew they'd been preserved through her suffering?

His heart clenched at the memory of Eva describing the workhouse—the casual cruelty, the stolen dignity. Now she endured similar horrors again because Billington had seen her worth to James.

No fortune was worth such a price.

James straightened his shoulders, setting the pen to paper with newfound resolve. He would choose love over fortune, Eva over legacy. A life without her, no matter how materially comfortable, would be hollow and meaningless.

"I'll rebuild," he muttered, pressing the nib to parchment. "We'll rebuild together."

The image of Eva's face filled his mind again—not the smiling, carefree Eva from their afternoons in Hyde Park, but Eva as he'd last glimpsed her, being dragged through the shop. The fear in her eyes had been eclipsed by something more powerful—a fierce determination that refused to be broken.

If she could face Billington's cruelty with such courage, how could he do any less?

His hand moved across the page, forming the first letter of his name. The Pembroke docks would pass to Billington, but James would not let Eva become another victim of circumstance and powerful men's games. Her unwavering spirit had awakened his own courage, compelling him to act rather than merely lament.

The pen scratched against parchment as he prepared to complete his signature.

The door to his study burst open with a crash that made him jump, the pen skittering across the page.

"Lord Pembroke! Stop!"

A figure stood silhouetted in the doorway, breathless from running.

RESOLVE

James blinked, as he grabbed the pen and poised it above the document. The man before him was perhaps a few years older than himself, with light brown hair and an expensive but practical coat that spoke of mercantile success rather than inherited wealth. Though dishevelled from apparent haste, he carried himself with the confidence of someone accustomed to being heard.

"Who are you?" James demanded, rising from his chair. "How did you get past my staff?"

"My name is William Ansley," the man said, stepping forward and catching his breath. "I'm a merchant from Liverpool. Your butler tried to stop me, but I told him it was a matter of life and death—which it is." His hazel eyes fell to the papers on the desk. "And I beg you, don't sign those documents."

James stiffened. "How do you know about these papers?"

"I don't know what they contain exactly," William admitted, "but I've spent enough time investigating Marcus Billington to know his methods. Whatever he's forcing you to sign will benefit him at your expense—and at Eva's."

"Eva?" James circled the desk, scrutinising the stranger more carefully. "You know Evangeline Hartwell?"

William's expression softened. "I've been searching for her for nearly ten years. We were children together on the SS Lydia when it sank. She told me stories about the stars and Boston Harbour." A hint of a smile touched his lips. "She had these golden curls that caught the sunlight, even on the stormiest days."

James felt a jolt of recognition. "The boy who taught her about constellations ..." he murmured, remembering Eva's stories of her friend from the ship. "She mentioned you."

"She spoke of me?" William's face brightened momentarily before turning grave again. "I never stopped looking for her. After I was rescued, I made inquiries at every port, checked survivor lists from other lifeboats. My father thought I was obsessed, but I couldn't forget her."

James gestured to a chair. "Please, sit. Tell me everything."

William sank into the offered seat, running a hand through his windblown hair. "I've been tracking Billington's operations for months. He's been systematically targeting your family's shipping interests, hasn't he?"

James nodded grimly. "For nearly three years. Ships mysteriously diverted, cargo spoiled, investors suddenly withdrawing support. We couldn't prove anything until now."

"It's all connected," William leaned forward urgently. "But there's something—someone—you need to know about. The reason I'm here." He took a deep breath. "Captain Thomas Hartwell is alive."

James froze. "Eva's father? That's impossible. She saw him go down with the ship."

"Not quite," William said. "He was pulled from the water by a fishing vessel the morning after the storm. He'd suffered a severe head injury and had no memory of who he was. The sailors found his papers and that brass compass he always wore. They took him to Liverpool Royal Infirmary."

James paced the study, trying to absorb this revelation. "Eva only just learned he might be alive. A sailor told her ..."

"Jameson," William nodded. "I met him too. He recognised the Captain when they brought him in. Thomas spent years recovering at the hospital, eventually working there as an orderly while his memory slowly returned."

"And now?" James asked, hope rising in his chest.

"He's regained most of his memory and has been searching for Eva just as desperately as I've been." William's expression hardened. "But that's not all. In the process, he uncovered evidence of corruption involving workhouse operators and factory owners. He's been gathering testimonies and documents proving that Billington has been illegally trafficking workhouse inmates, especially children, forcing them into labour contracts at his factories."

James slammed his fist against the desk. "He's holding Eva in one of those factories right now, threatening to harm her unless I sign over my family's shipping business."

"Then it's exactly as I feared," William said grimly. "Billington must have discovered Eva's connection to you and saw an opportunity to finally seize your docks—the one piece of your business empire he couldn't sabotage through conventional means."

James stared at the papers before him, understanding the full scope of Billington's scheme for the first time. "We must find Mr Hartwell. With his evidence—"

"He's already on his way to London," William interrupted. "I received word yesterday that he's bringing everything he's gathered to the authorities. But he doesn't know about Eva's kidnapping. He believes she's still working at the dressmaker's shop."

James returned to his chair, mind racing. "How soon can he arrive?"

"He will be here by daybreak I hope," William replied. "But I fear that may be too late. If Billington suspects his larger operation might be exposed, he could move Eva or ..." He didn't finish the thought.

"Or worse," James completed grimly. "We can't wait for Mr Hartwell. We need to act now."

James rose from his chair with newfound resolve. "Every moment we delay puts Eva in greater danger." He strode to the window, watching the afternoon light begin its slow fade over London's skyline. "My sister believes she's being held at Billington's textile mill in Whitechapel—a dreadful place by all accounts."

"And you trust your sister's hunch?" William asked.

"I do." James said stoically.

William stood beside him, jaw set with determination. "Then we go to Whitechapel tonight. The two of us."

"Just the two of us?" James turned, studying William's face.

"Who else can we trust? The authorities? They're likely in Billington's pocket. Your family?"

"My family has made their position on Eva very clear ..." James said sombrely. "Besides, a larger group would draw attention." He crossed to a cabinet in the corner of the study and unlocked it, revealing a small pistol. "My father always kept this for protection. I've never had cause to use it."

"Let's pray we won't need it tonight," William said, though his expression suggested he didn't believe his own words.

James tucked the weapon into his coat. "I'll have my carriage prepared. We should dress practically—dark clothes, sturdy boots. Nothing that marks us as gentlemen."

"I have my traveling clothes still," William replied. "They'll serve well enough."

As dusk settled over London, the two men met in the courtyard. James barely recognised the merchant in his rough coat and cap, all signs of his prosperity hidden away. James himself had changed into his oldest riding clothes, a dark scarf wrapped around his neck to obscure his face.

"My driver is loyal," James said as they climbed into the waiting carriage. "He knows only that we have urgent business in Whitechapel."

The carriage lurched forward, beginning its journey through London's darkening streets. Inside, the men spoke in low voices, planning their approach.

"The factory has a night watchman," James explained, "but the main workforce is locked inside from dusk till dawn. Scarlett discovered the workers sleep on the upper floors when they're not at the machines."

William leaned forward. "Any weak points in the building?"

"There's a loading bay at the rear where materials come in. Less visible from the street." James traced the route in the air with his finger. "And the foreman's office has a separate entrance—likely where they keep keys to the dormitories."

The journey seemed interminable, the carriage navigating through progressively narrower and more squalid streets. Both men fell silent, lost in their own thoughts as the gaslights grew fewer and the shadows deeper.

"We were just children when the ship went down," William said suddenly, staring out at the passing darkness. "But even then, there was something about Eva—a courage that made others brave. She told me stories about the stars to keep me from being afraid during the storm."

James felt a twist of emotion in his chest. "She hasn't changed. She still finds beauty in the darkest places."

Midnight came and went. The streets emptied of all but the most desperate souls. As they approached Whitechapel, the smell of the factories—coal smoke, chemicals, and unwashed bodies—permeated the air.

"It will be nearly two by the time we reach it," James said, checking his pocket watch in the dim light. "Perfect timing—the night watchman should be at his sleepiest."

William nodded, squaring his shoulders. "Then let's bring Eva home."

RECKONING

*A*rchibald Mountforth paced the length of Billington's office, his boots leaving grimy tracks across the expensive carpet. The factory's midnight silence would have been complete if not for the distant hum of machines still running on the night shift—a constant reminder of Billington's profitable empire. Mountforth's gaze fell upon the papers sprawled across the mahogany desk, illuminated by a single gas lamp.

"You're certain of this information?" he demanded, jabbing a finger at the hastily scrawled note.

Billington sat behind his desk, face half in shadow. "My source in the Pembroke household has never been wrong before. Lord James and this merchant fellow—Ansley—they're on their way here now." He slid another paper forward. "And this report from Liverpool confirms the worst. Captain Thomas Hartwell is alive and gathering evidence against us both."

The name struck Mountforth like a physical blow. "Hartwell," he spat. "The whelp's father?"

"Indeed." Billington's voice remained level, though his fingers betrayed him, drumming an agitated rhythm on the desktop. "It seems our operation faces threats from multiple fronts."

Mountforth tugged at his collar, suddenly feeling the night air thick and stifling. "What does he know?"

"Everything apparently." Billington's lips thinned to a harsh line. "The workhouse escapes, the labour contracts, the children we've moved between facilities. Names, dates, witnesses."

Something cold slithered down Mountforth's spine. Witnesses meant testimonies. Testimonies meant trials. Trials meant the gallows. He'd seen enough men hang in his lifetime to know precisely how long it took to die on the end of a rope.

"We need to eliminate the evidence," Mountforth muttered, more to himself than to his business partner. His mind raced through possibilities, each more desperate than the last.

Billington rose from his chair, straightening his waistcoat with practiced precision. "I've already sent for additional guards. When Pembroke and Ansley arrive, we'll be waiting. Once I have the signed shipping documents, we'll dispose of our ... complications."

But Mountforth barely heard him. A plan was forming in his mind—crude, brutal, and final. "Fire," he whispered.

"What did you say?" Billington paused, glancing back.

"Nothing."

Before Billington could press further, Mountforth stormed from the office, his heart hammering against his ribs. The corridor outside stretched long and dark, lit only by occasional gas lamps that cast more shadows than light. Two of his most trusted ruffians—former workhouse guards who'd followed him into Billington's employ—stood waiting near the stairs.

"Masters. Burke. With me," he ordered, not breaking stride.

They followed without question, accustomed to his harsh commands. Down the narrow service stairwell they descended, past the main factory floor where exhausted women and children hunched over thundering looms, into the dank basement that reeked of coal dust and machine oil.

"We need to start a fire," Mountforth announced, watching their expressions carefully. "A controlled burn at first—small blazes at strategic points that will grow together. The evidence must be destroyed completely."

Burke, the burlier of the two, shifted uncomfortably. "Sir, there's nearly sixty souls working tonight, plus them sleeping upstairs—"

"I'm aware of the numbers," Mountforth cut him off, eyes narrowing. "Are you developing a conscience at this late stage, Burke?"

The man lowered his gaze. "No, sir."

"Good. Masters, fetch the kerosene from the supply closet. Burke, gather rags and tinder." He pulled his pocket watch out, flipping open the case. "Pembroke and his companion will be here within the hour. We need the fire well established by then."

As his men hurried to comply, Mountforth surveyed the basement. Ancient wooden support beams ran the length of the ceiling, perfectly positioned to carry flames up through the building's core. The ventilation shafts would draw the fire upward like chimneys, trapping the sleeping workers on the upper floors. Including Eva Hartwell.

A smile tugged at his lips, his first genuine one in days. How fitting that the girl who'd escaped his workhouse through fire would meet her end the same way. Poetic, really.

When Masters returned with the kerosene, Mountforth directed him to the far corners of the basement, where the wooden beams met stone foundations. "Pour it generously," he instructed. "Ensure it soaks into the wood."

Within minutes, the acrid smell of kerosene permeated the basement. Burke had assembled piles of oil-soaked rags beneath each treated beam.

"Light them," Mountforth commanded, stepping back to watch.

The first match struck with a hiss, its flame momentarily illuminating Burke's hesitant face before he touched it to the nearest rag. Fire blossomed immediately, greedily consuming the fuel and licking up the wooden beam. Masters followed suit at the opposite corner, and soon four separate fires burned steadily, the flames growing higher with each passing moment.

Mountforth felt a surge of satisfaction as the first wisps of smoke began to curl toward the ceiling, seeking escape through the ancient building's cracks and seams. Above, the machinery continued its rhythmic clatter, the workers yet unaware of the death creeping toward them.

"Now the offices," he instructed, leading his men back up the stairs. Heat already pulsed behind them like a living thing. "We need to ensure the records are completely destroyed."

They emerged onto the main floor, where a haze of smoke had begun to gather near the ceiling. A few workers glanced up in confusion, nostrils flaring at the acrid scent.

"Keep working!" Mountforth bellowed, silencing their murmurs with practiced authority.

Making their way toward the administrative wing, Mountforth paused to touch flame to a stack of cotton bales. The material caught with shocking speed, flames leaping shoulder-high in seconds. Screams erupted from the nearest workers as sparks showered across their workstations.

"Sir!" Burke called out, pointing toward the growing inferno. "It's spreading faster than we planned!"

Mountforth ignored him, continuing toward Billington's office with single-minded determination. The smoke thickened with each step, rolling down the corridor in choking waves. From somewhere behind came the sound of splintering wood as fire-weakened beams gave way.

He threw open the office door to find Billington standing by the window, face contorted with rage.

"What have you done, you madman?" Billington shouted, gesturing wildly at the smoke pouring beneath the door. "This wasn't the plan!"

"Plans change," Mountforth replied coldly. "The evidence burns as we speak."

"Along with my entire investment!" Billington lunged forward, seizing Mountforth by the lapels. "You've destroyed everything!"

Mountforth staggered backward under the assault, unprepared for Billington's fury. His heel caught on the carpet edge, sending both men crashing to the floor. Billington's fist connected with Mountforth's jaw, sending pain lancing through his skull.

"You fool!" Billington snarled, punctuating each word with another blow. "We could have managed this! Now we'll hang for murder!"

Mountforth tasted blood, metallic and warm. Through the window behind Billington's head, he could see orange flames engulfing the factory floor, far larger than he'd anticipated. The fire had found the stores of cotton and wool, creating an inferno that roared like a living beast.

For the first time, a flicker of doubt crept into his mind. Perhaps he'd miscalculated.

FIRE

"Faster!" James urged the coachman, his knuckles white against the carriage door. The wheels clattered over cobblestones, each jolt a reminder of precious seconds ticking away. "Take the alley past Bishopsgate—it's quicker!"

William braced himself against the seat opposite, his merchant's finery exchanged for practical attire. "The factory will be guarded. We must approach with caution."

"Forget caution," James muttered. "Eva's in there."

The carriage lurched around a corner, narrowly missing a fruit seller's cart. James caught a glimpse of Whitechapel's skyline through the window—a forest of chimneys belching smoke into the night sky. Among them, one plume seemed darker, angrier.

"Something's wrong," William said, following James' gaze. "That smoke—"

The words died in his throat as they rounded the final corner. The eastern sky blazed orange, a hellish backdrop to Billington's textile mill. Flames licked from windows on the lower floors, black smoke pouring from the upper stories.

"No," James whispered. "Dear God, no."

Before the carriage fully stopped, James flung open the door and leapt to the street. The heat struck him like a physical blow, singeing his eyebrows even from fifty yards away. A crowd had gathered—neighbours, passers-by, workers who'd escaped—their faces ghoulishly illuminated by the inferno.

"Eva!" James screamed, his voice lost in the roar of the flames and the cacophony of shouts around him. "EVA!"

William caught up, gripping James' arm. "We need to find another entrance. The main doors are blocked."

A woman staggered past, her face streaked with soot, coughing violently. James caught her arm. "The upper floors—are there still people inside?"

She nodded, eyes wide with terror. "The children—they sleep on the top floor. The stairs are gone."

James felt the blood drain from his face. That's where they'd keep Eva—isolated, away from exits.

"There!" William pointed to a side entrance where workers were streaming out, many collapsing once they reached safety. "Service stairs might still be intact."

They pushed against the tide of fleeing humanity, deaf to warnings shouted at their backs. The doorway gaped like the mouth of hell, belching heat and toxic smoke. James pulled his neckerchief over his nose and mouth, gesturing for William to do the same.

"Stay low," James instructed, dropping to a crouch as they entered. The smoke hung in layers, thicker toward the ceiling. The ground floor was a maze of burning looms and workstations, cotton bales feeding the flames like kindling.

"This way!" William pointed toward a narrow corridor where fewer flames had taken hold. "There must be stairs at the back!"

They crawled forward, eyes streaming, lungs burning with each breath. The heat pressed down like a physical weight, the air shimmering around them. Twice they were forced to change course as burning debris crashed down from above.

A terrible splintering sound rent the air as a section of ceiling collapsed twenty feet ahead, sparks erupting skyward. James felt despair clutch at his heart. Were they already too late?

"James!" William's voice cut through his darkening thoughts. "Look there!"

Through the billowing smoke, a staircase appeared, its wooden treads still intact though flames licked at the lower steps. Without hesitation, James lunged forward, taking the stairs two at a time. The banister was hot enough to blister his palm when he grabbed it for balance.

The second floor was a vision from Dante's Inferno. Flames danced across work tables where hours earlier women had bent over sewing machines. The air was thick with floating embers and ash, visibility reduced to mere feet.

"EVA!" James called again, his voice cracking. "Can anyone hear me?"

A faint sound answered—not Eva's voice, but human nonetheless. Following it, they found a young boy huddled beneath an overturned cart, paralysed with fear.

"Where are the others?" William asked, helping the child to his feet.

"Top floor," the boy coughed. "The dormitory. Miss Eva—she was trying to get them out."

James' heart soared and plummeted simultaneously. She was alive—but still trapped above.

"Go with him," James told William, nodding toward the boy. "Get him out."

"You can't go up there alone," William protested. "The structure won't hold much longer."

"I'm not leaving without her." James' tone brooked no argument. "If I'm not back in ten minutes—"

"I'll come after you," William finished, already guiding the boy toward the stairs they'd ascended.

James pressed on, finding a narrow service stairwell at the far end of the floor. The treads groaned ominously beneath his weight, weakened by the heat. At the landing, he paused, the smoke so thick he could barely see his hand before his face.

Dropping to his knees, he crawled forward into the third-floor dormitory. Rows of iron cots lined the walls, all empty. The far side of the room was already consumed by fire, the ceiling beginning to sag dangerously.

"Eva!" he called, his voice now a rasp. "Where are you?"

He pushed forward toward the wall of flame that divided the room. Somewhere beyond that fiery barrier was Eva—the woman he loved, the soul he couldn't bear to lose.

FIERCER THAN FIRE

*E*va clutched Sarah's small hand, eyes stinging from acrid smoke as she counted heads for the third time. Four children—all present, all terrified. The youngest no more than six. Behind them, flames consumed the dormitory's far wall, crackling like demonic laughter.

"We'll make it through this," Eva assured them, her voice steady despite the inferno's roar. "Remember what I told you? We're fiercer than any fire."

She'd learned that from her father, a lifetime ago on a storm-tossed ship. Now she needed that same courage.

"Everyone hold hands. Don't let go." Eva crouched to meet their eyes. "Sarah, you're behind me. Then Daniel, May, and Tommy at the back. We stay together."

The children formed their chain, faces streaked with soot and tears. Eva had already tried the main staircase—a death trap of collapsed timbers and flames. Their only hope lay through the back corridors where the factory machinery might provide some protection from the spreading fire.

"The service passage runs alongside the spinning room," Eva explained, remembering her careful mental mapping of the building during her captivity. "If we can reach it, there's a metal staircase for the mechanics."

She led them into the smoke-filled hallway, keeping low where the air remained breathable. The children mimicked her movements instinctively, a small, determined army crawling through hell.

A tremendous crack split the air as a support beam crashed down ten feet ahead, sending up a fountain of embers. May screamed, trying to pull away, but Eva steadied her.

"It's all right," she soothed, though nothing was all right. "That path's blocked, but I know another way."

They veered left into the spinning room, a vast chamber filled with massive iron machines. The heat here was nearly unbearable, the wooden floorboards hot beneath their palms and knees. Eva navigated between the hulking shapes, using them as shields against falling debris.

The children's coughing grew worse, their movements slowing. Eva fought her own burning lungs, each breath a battle against the smoke threatening to overwhelm them.

"Keep moving," she urged. "See that doorway? That's our way out."

Halfway across the room, little Tommy collapsed. Eva immediately backtracked, lifting the boy despite her exhausted muscles screaming in protest.

"Almost there," she whispered, though she wasn't certain it was true. The factory had become a labyrinth of flame and shadow, familiar landmarks transformed into nightmarish obstacles.

They reached a narrow passageway between two massive looms. Eva pushed the children through one by one, then squeezed through herself, still carrying Thomas. His small body felt impossibly heavy against her chest.

The service corridor beyond was mercifully clearer, though

smoke still swirled around them. Eva could make out the metal staircase at the far end—their salvation.

"Just a little further," she encouraged, her voice hoarse. "Then down the stairs and—"

A tremendous crash drowned her words as part of the ceiling collapsed behind them, sealing off their retreat. May screamed again, and even stoic Daniel began to sob.

"Eyes forward," Eva commanded, refusing to let panic take hold. "Don't look back."

They stumbled forward, the metal staircase tantalisingly close now. Eva's legs trembled with exhaustion, her eyes burning so fiercely she could barely see. Thomas stirred weakly in her arms, a good sign.

Through the smoke, a silhouette appeared on the staircase. A man, coming upward against all reason. Eva's heart leapt painfully in her chest.

"Help!" she called, her voice barely a rasp. "We're here!"

DESPERATION

"Eva!" James shouted, his voice barely audible over the inferno's roar. The heat pressed against his skin like a physical force, each breath scorching his lungs. "Eva!"

William stumbled beside him, handkerchief pressed to his mouth. They'd split up after rescuing the boy—William taking him to safety while James pushed deeper into the burning factory. Now William had returned, refusing to let James face the flames alone.

"We need to reach the upper floor!" James coughed violently, eyes streaming from the smoke.

A support beam crashed through the ceiling ten feet ahead, sending up a fountain of embers that forced them back. William grabbed James' sleeve, pointing to a narrow passage between massive iron machines.

"The machinery room!" William shouted. "It might be more stable—metal doesn't burn as quickly!"

They ducked low, beneath the worst of the smoke, and pushed forward. James' fine wool coat was singed with dozens of tiny burn holes, his hands blackened with soot. None of it mattered. Nothing mattered except finding Eva.

The machinery room was an apocalyptic landscape of shadows and flame, the hulking machines transformed into monstrous silhouettes. Heat radiated from the metal contraptions, making the air shimmer.

"There!" William pointed toward a service corridor barely visible through the smoke. "That must lead to the dormitories!"

James' heart hammered against his ribs, a desperate rhythm that matched his racing thoughts. Every second counted. Every moment spent searching was another moment Eva might be losing her battle against the flames.

A memory flashed in his mind—Eva laughing in the sunlight of Hyde Park, her golden curls catching the light as she read from his father's poetry book. The thought of never seeing that smile again drove him forward with renewed desperation.

AMIDST THE FLAMES

The outline of a man materialised through the dense smoke, his silhouette growing larger as he approached. Eva clutched Tommy closer to her chest, urging the other children behind her. Her heart faltered as recognition dawned.

"Well, well. What have we here?"

Mr Mountforth's voice slithered through the chaos, that same cold, calculating tone that had haunted Eva's nightmares for years. His face appeared ghostly, illuminated by the dancing flames behind him, eyes glinting with malice.

"Trying to escape again, are we, Miss Hartwell?" He stepped closer, limping slightly. "Always the little hero."

Eva's throat closed with terror. After everything—the shipwreck, the workhouse, her escape to London, building a new life—it all came down to this moment, trapped between fire and the man who'd tormented her for years.

"Stay back," she managed, her voice steadier than she felt. "These children need to get out."

Mr Mountforth sneered. "Always giving orders. Did you think I wouldn't find you? Did you think—"

"Get away from my daughter."

The new voice—deep, commanding, achingly familiar—cut through the roar of the flames like a ship's bell through fog. Eva's heart stopped. It couldn't be. It simply couldn't.

A tall figure emerged from the shadows behind Mountforth. Broad-shouldered and straight-backed despite the years, his face weathered but unmistakable. The brass compass still hung at his throat, catching the firelight.

"Father?" The word escaped Eva's lips as barely more than a breath.

Captain Thomas Hartwell stood before them, solid and real. His eyes—her eyes—blazed with fury as he stared down Mountforth.

"I said, get away from my daughter."

Mountforth's face contorted with rage and confusion. "Impossible. You drowned with that ship."

"The sea wasn't ready for me." Father's gaze flicked briefly to Eva, softening for just a moment before hardening again. "Mr Ansley's message reached me just in time. Seems God had other plans tonight."

Eva couldn't move, couldn't breathe. The children huddled against her legs, wide-eyed at the confrontation unfolding before them. Her father—alive, standing mere feet away. The father she'd mourned, whose face she'd struggled to keep clear in her memory as the years passed.

Mountforth lunged suddenly, producing a knife from his coat. "You should have stayed dead."

Her father sidestepped with the agility of a man who'd spent decades on shifting decks. He caught Mountforth's wrist mid-strike, twisting until the knife clattered to the floor.

"Eva, take the children. Now!" Her father commanded, not looking away from Mountforth.

She hesitated, torn between obeying and fear of losing him again.

"Go!" he shouted as Mountforth broke free, tackling him backwards.

Eva guided the children toward the metal staircase, pausing at the top. Below, through gaps in the smoke, she glimpsed uniformed figures gathering outside—police, waiting to enter the burning building.

The two men grappled violently, stumbling toward the edge of the collapsing floor. Father's fist connected with Mountforth's jaw, sending him staggering back. Mountforth caught himself against a support beam, blood trickling from his split lip.

"It's over, Mountforth," her father shouted over the roar of flames. "The authorities have your records. They know about the children you've exploited, the lives you've destroyed."

Mountforth's face twisted. "They know nothing. And they never will." He charged again, catching her father around the middle.

They crashed against the far wall, dangerously close to where the floor had already given way, revealing the inferno below. Father broke Mountforth's grip, shoving him back, but the workhouse master's boot caught on a protruding board. He stumbled, arms wind milling as he fought for balance at the very edge.

Time seemed to slow. Mountforth teetered, half his body suspended over the abyss of flame and falling debris. His eyes widened with genuine fear for perhaps the first time in his life.

Her father lunged forward, hand outstretched. "Take my hand!"

Eva couldn't believe it. After everything Mountforth had done, her father was trying to save him.

"I'd rather burn," Mountforth spat, even as his fingers scrabbled for purchase on the charred floorboards. His eyes locked with Eva's across the room, filled with hatred to the last.

The floor beneath him gave way with a terrible splintering

crack. Her father threw himself backwards as Mountforth disappeared into the inferno below, his scream lost amid the building's groans.

Her father stood frozen for a moment before turning toward Eva. Ten years of separation hung between them like the smoke, heavy with grief, questions and disbelief.

"Evangeline," he whispered, her full name on his lips a benediction.

The floor shuddered beneath them, and a beam crashed down nearby, sending up a shower of sparks.

"We need to go. **NOW!**" Her father said, crossing over to her in three long strides.

Eva nodded, her body moving on instinct while her mind still struggled to comprehend the miracle before her. Her father was alive. Her father had found her.

POWERLESS

*B*illington fled through the winding back passage of his factory, the polished brogues that had carried him through London's finest drawing rooms now slipping on the grimy stone floor. Sweat beaded his brow—not from the heat of the inferno above, but from the fear gripping his chest.

The plan had collapsed spectacularly. Hartwell alive and in London. Mountforth setting his own factory ablaze. The Pembroke boy refusing to break. The carefully constructed scheme, years in the making, reduced to ash as thoroughly as the building behind him.

No matter. He still had options. Always options.

He patted the documents in his breast pocket—forged deeds and blackmail material that would suffice to rebuild elsewhere. Amsterdam, perhaps. Or New York. Somewhere the Pembroke name held no sway.

The narrow corridor opened into his private loading dock, where the Thames lapped against stone. His personal skiff waited, tethered and ready. Billington had always prepared for contingencies. A man in his position—a man who dealt in flesh and misery—required escape routes.

"Barrett!" he hissed at the figure hunched by the boat. "Cast off immediately."

His man scrambled to obey, fumbling with the rope. Billington strode toward freedom, already tasting the salt air that would carry him to the merchant vessel waiting downriver. By dawn, he'd be in international waters. By week's end, halfway to America with a new name and sufficient capital to begin again.

He reached the edge of the dock, one foot already extended toward the bobbing skiff, when movement caught his eye.

At first, just shadows shifting. Then a lantern flared, illuminating the ring of men blocking the river passage.

Dock workers. Dozens of them. Their faces grim, arms crossed over broad chests built from years of hauling cargo. Pembroke's men.

"Looking to take a pleasure cruise, Mr Billington?" The foreman stepped forward, a burly man with calloused hands and cold eyes. "Afraid the river's closed to the likes of you tonight."

Billington's heart hammered against his ribs. He glanced right—more workers. Left—the same wall of humanity. Behind—smoke billowed from windows as his factory burned, silhouetting police officers closing in.

"This is outrageous," Billington sputtered, drawing himself up. "I demand passage. I own half the shipping in this port!"

A ripple of dark laughter moved through the gathered men.

"Funny thing about that," said the foreman, stepping closer. "Lord Pembroke owns the other half. And unlike you, he pays fair wages. Treats his men with respect." He spat at Billington's feet. "We know what goes on in that factory of yours. The children. The conditions. My sister's boy disappeared from a workhouse last year. Ended up in your textile mill."

Panic rose in Billington's throat. These men weren't merely blocking his escape—they wanted blood. "I can pay you," he said, reaching for his purse. "More than Pembroke ever could. Twenty pounds each to look the other way."

The foreman's weathered face hardened. "Some things can't be bought, Mr Billington. Some wrongs can't be paid off."

The circle tightened. Behind him, Barrett had already surrendered to a police officer, hands raised in submission.

Billington backed against a stack of crates, cornered like a rat. His kingdom of exploitation and suffering had crumbled in a single night. The very workers he'd deemed disposable, interchangeable cogs in his machine of profit, now stood between him and freedom.

For the first time in his adult life, Marcus Billington found himself utterly powerless.

ESCAPE

*E*va barely had time to look at her father before a deafening crack echoed through the burning factory. She whirled around to see a massive wooden beam descending from the ceiling, splintering as it fell. Little Tommy stood frozen directly beneath it, his eyes wide with terror.

"Tommy!" Eva lunged forward, shoving the child with all her might. He tumbled safely into her father's arms just as the beam crashed down, pinning Eva's leg beneath its smouldering weight. White-hot pain shot through her calf. She bit back a scream, not wanting to frighten the children further.

"Eva!" Her father's voice cracked with anguish.

"Get them out!" Eva commanded through gritted teeth, gesturing to the four terrified children. "The service stairs are still clear. I'll find another way."

Thomas hesitated, torn between his daughter and the innocent lives in his care.

"Go!" Eva insisted. "I'll be right behind you."

A silent understanding passed between them—the certainty that they would not lose each other again. With a curt nod, Thomas gathered the children and rushed toward the stairwell, glancing back only once before disappearing through the smoke.

Eva tugged frantically at her trapped leg, each movement sending shards of agony through her body. The beam wouldn't budge. Around her, the fire consumed the factory's bones, turning wood to ash and metal to liquid. The air grew thinner with each gasping breath.

James and William burst into the machinery room, their faces streaked with soot, lungs burning from the smoke. The massive iron contraptions stood like sentinels in the inferno, their metal frames glowing red with heat.

"Eva!" James called, his voice hoarse.

Through gaps in the billowing smoke, he spotted her—golden hair dulled by ash, hands bloodied from attempting to free herself from beneath a fallen beam. The sight knocked the wind from his lungs more effectively than any smoke.

"There!" William pointed, already moving toward a narrow path through the debris.

James didn't hesitate. He launched himself over burning rubble, heedless of the blistering heat that seared through his clothes.

"Eva! I'm coming!" he shouted, scrambling over twisted metal and splintered wood.

She looked up, disbelief and hope warring across her soot-stained face. "James?"

He reached her side, dropping to his knees beside the massive beam. Its weight would require three men to lift under normal circumstances. But these were not normal circumstances. With strength born of desperation, James braced his shoulder against the smouldering wood.

"When I lift, pull yourself free," he commanded, muscles already straining against the impossible weight.

Eva nodded, preparing herself for more pain.

James heaved upward, veins standing out on his neck, a guttural cry tearing from his throat. The beam rose just enough. Eva dragged herself backward, her face contorted in agony. William appeared through the smoke, helping to pull her clear.

"James, let go!" William shouted. "The whole structure's giving way!"

James released the beam, stumbling backward as it crashed down again. The impact sent tremors through the already unstable floor. A sickening crack reverberated beneath them. The floorboards splintered, revealing the blazing inferno below.

"Move!" James grabbed Eva's arm, trying to drag her toward safety, but the floor tilted beneath them like the deck of a sinking ship. Eva slid toward the widening gap, her fingers clawing for purchase on the smooth wooden boards.

James lunged for her hand, catching it just as the floor gave way completely. They hung suspended—Eva dangling over the fiery chasm below, James stretched across the crumbling edge, his grip the only thing between her and certain death.

"Hold on!" he cried, his fingers slipping against hers.

Eva's eyes locked with his, filled not with fear but with a terrible acceptance. "James, you have to let go or we'll both fall."

"Never," he snarled, tightening his grip even as splinters drove into his palm. "I will not lose you."

The remaining floorboards groaned, threatening to collapse under James' weight. William scrambled to help, but he was too far away, separated by a widening gulf of flame.

Just as James felt his strength failing, a commanding voice cut through the roar of the fire.

"Hold fast, lad!"

A strong hand gripped James' shoulder, and another reached down past him. Captain Thomas Hartwell had returned, his face set with grim determination as he extended his arm toward his daughter.

"Eva, take my hand!"

With a desperate lunge, Eva caught her father's outstretched hand. Together, Thomas and James hauled her up from the jaws of destruction, the three of them collapsing in a heap on the small island of stability that remained.

"We need to move. **NOW**," Thomas ordered, already helping Eva to her feet.

William pointed toward a service door half-hidden behind a loom. "That way! It leads to the back stairs!"

Thomas scooped Eva into his arms despite her protests. "Save your strength, little one. We're not safe yet."

They staggered through the doorway just as the remainder of the floor collapsed behind them, sending a blast of heat and sparks up their backs. The narrow service stairs offered their only escape route, spiralling downward through relatively clean air.

"The children?" Eva gasped, clutching her father's jacket.

"Safe outside with the constables," Thomas assured her. "You saved them all."

They emerged into the cool night air like souls escaping purgatory, gulping in great lungful's of clean oxygen. Fire engines clanged in the distance, their bells a chorus of salvation. Police officers swarmed the area, arresting Billington's men and helping the rescued workers.

Eva slumped against her father, watching the factory burn. The pain in her leg seemed distant now, overshadowed by the miracle of survival—and reunion.

"Eva." James stood before her, his face blackened with soot, eyes blazing with an intensity that matched the inferno behind him. "I thought I'd lost you."

She reached for his hand, her fingers intertwining with his. "Not yet," she whispered.

THE CAPTAIN'S LOST DAUGHTER

Thomas looked between them, recognition dawning on his weathered face. "So this is the man who came for my daughter."

James straightened, meeting the captain's gaze. "I would do it again, sir. A thousand times over."

A commotion near the docks drew their attention. Officers led a handcuffed Billington through the crowd of liberated workers. His once-immaculate suit hung in tatters, his arrogant facade shattered.

"It's over," William said, stepping to Eva's side. "His operations are exposed. The constables are already moving to free the workers in his other factories."

"William ... Is it ... But I ..." Eva stepped toward him, overwhelmed.

William burst into a big smile, the same he'd had at twelve. "It's me. It's a very *very* long story. And I think we all need a bath before that."

As dawn broke over London, pale light illuminated the smoke-filled sky. The factory—once a prison of cruelty and exploitation—now burned away to ash, its destruction somehow cleansing.

Eva leaned against her father, James' hand still firmly in hers, and watched the sunrise paint the city gold. In that moment, surrounded by those who had risked everything to save her, Eva finally understood what her father had taught her years ago.

She was indeed fiercer than any storm, stronger than any fire. And she was no longer alone.

REUNION

*E*va sat on the edge of a hospital bed, her leg throbbing beneath the hastily applied bandages. The hospital bustled around her, a cacophony of pain and urgency. Nurses rushed between beds with arms full of linens, doctors barked orders, and the moans of the injured created a sorrowful chorus that echoed through the high-ceilinged ward. Through the windows, the orange glow of the still-burning factory painted the night sky, a monument to both horror and liberation.

William had disappeared into the crowd outside, promising to return after helping with the rescue efforts. "There are still people who need help," he'd said, squeezing her hand before vanishing into the smoke-filled night.

A weary doctor had assessed her burns, his fingers gentle but clinical as they probed the angry red flesh of her calf and the blistered skin of her forearms. "These will heal," he'd muttered, "but they'll leave scars."

"I've had worse," Eva had replied, earning a curious glance from the man before he moved on to more critical patients.

Now, as a nurse dabbed salve onto her wounds, Eva felt a sharp sting that made her gasp despite her determination to remain stoic. The pain broke through her careful composure, and suddenly the events of the past days crashed over her like a tidal wave. She trembled, her shoulders hunching forward as her body seemed to remember every terror it had endured.

"I'll fetch you some tea with laudanum," the nurse said, misinterpreting her shaking for pain alone.

Eva nodded absently, her eyes seeking James through the crowded ward. He stood by the wall, his tall frame unmistakable, even in the dim light. Their gazes met across the room, and he offered a small, reassuring smile before glancing toward the figure seated beside her.

Her father.

Captain Thomas Hartwell sat perfectly still, his weathered hands clasped together, knuckles white with tension. He hadn't spoken more than a few necessary words since they'd arrived at the hospital, as though afraid his voice might shatter the fragile reality of their reunion.

"You look like her," he said suddenly, breaking the silence between them. "Your mother."

Eva turned to him, drinking in his features—the familiar green eyes now framed by deeper lines, the strong jaw softened slightly with age, the dark hair now streaked with silver at the temples. He was both exactly as she remembered and completely transformed.

"People used to say that," she whispered. "Before ..."

"Before I lost you." His voice cracked on the final word. "Eva, I searched for you. For years. They told me you'd drowned when the lifeboat capsized. I couldn't ... I couldn't accept it. But the evidence ..."

"And I thought you'd been swallowed by the sea," Eva said, a small, sad smile touching her lips. "We've been ghosts to each other."

Her father reached out, his hand hovering uncertainly before gently taking hers. His palm was calloused, bearing new scars she didn't recognise. "I remember fragments of those early days. The doctors said I might never regain all my memories of the shipwreck. But I never forgot you or your mother."

"The brass compass," Eva said. "The sailor who told me you might be alive, he mentioned it."

"I was still wearing it when they pulled me from the water." He reached inside his shirt collar and withdrew the familiar object, its brass surface dulled with age but intact. "It led me back to you, in a way."

Eva's vision blurred with tears. "I've carried pieces of our family too." She reached into her pocket, extracting the worn brass button Mrs Fisher had given her years ago. "To remember who I was. A kind woman who took me in after I washed ashore. She knew I'd need something to hold onto."

The nurse returned with tea, the medicinal smell of laudanum rising with the steam. Eva accepted it with murmured thanks, though she had no intention of drinking it. She needed her mind clear for this moment.

"I tried to make you proud," she said after the nurse departed. "Even in the workhouse, I remembered what you taught me—about being fiercer than the storm."

Her father's hand tightened around hers. "The workhouse." His voice hardened. "If I had known ..."

"You couldn't have," Eva said gently. "Just as I couldn't have known you were searching for me."

A cough from a nearby bed punctuated their conversation, reminding them of their surroundings. Through a gap in the crowd, Eva saw James speaking with a doctor, his gestures animated but controlled. Even now, dishevelled and soot-stained, he carried himself with dignity.

"He loves you," Her father observed, following her gaze.

Eva felt warmth rise to her cheeks. "He risked everything for me."

"As did you for those children." Pride gleamed in her father's eyes. "You truly are fiercer than any storm, Evangeline Hartwell."

The use of her full name brought fresh tears. How long had it been since anyone had addressed her properly, with the respect of her complete identity?

"Tell me," he said, his voice soft but urgent. "Tell me about the years I missed. Everything. I want to know the woman my daughter has become."

Eva took a deep breath, wincing slightly as it pulled at her burned skin. Where to begin? With Mrs Fisher's kindness? The workhouse's cruelty? The children she'd protected? Her escape to London and Miss Adelaide's generosity? Or perhaps with the moment a handsome lord had noticed a simple seamstress across a crowded shop?

"It's a long story," she warned.

Her father's smile was gentle, his eyes never leaving her face as though afraid she might disappear if he looked away. "We have time now. All the time in the world."

Outside, the first light of dawn was beginning to push back the darkness. The factory's flames had diminished to smouldering embers, and a new day was breaking over London—a day Eva had never expected to see, with people she had thought lost forever.

She squeezed her father's hand and began to speak.

IMPOSSIBLE CHOICES

James' mind churned with contradictions as he watched the medical team tend to Eva across the ward. Soot still blackened her golden curls, and angry red marks mottled her delicate hands where she'd battled the flames. Yet even now, reunited with her father and wounded, she carried herself with that quiet dignity that had first drawn him to her.

"We've managed to remove the debris from her wounds, my lord," the doctor murmured, adjusting his spectacles. "The burns are concerning but not life-threatening. With proper care and rest—"

"She'll have it," James said firmly. "Whatever she needs."

The doctor hesitated. "Forgive me, Lord Pembroke, but the matter of payment—"

"Is not a concern." James cut him off with a wave of his hand. "Send all accounts to my estate."

"Very good, sir."

As the doctor moved away, James caught sight of William entering the ward, his face grave despite the night's rescue. The two men exchanged a nod before William made his way to Eva and her father.

James remained where he stood, suddenly feeling like an intruder on their reunion. Captain Hartwell had lost ten years with his daughter; James had known her mere months. What right did he have to insert himself into this moment?

A constable approached, hat in hand. "Lord Pembroke, a word?"

James followed him to a quieter corner of the ward.

"We've apprehended Billington, sir. Found him trying to flee via the river docks."

Relief washed through James. "Thank God."

"Aye, sir. Though ..." The constable lowered his voice. "I feel I should warn you. Men like Billington—they've connections. Judges, magistrates. Money has a way of talking loudly in the courts."

"I'm well aware," James said, his jaw tightening. "And what of Mountforth?"

"No sign yet, sir. If he was still inside when the east wing collapsed ..." The constable left the implication hanging.

James nodded grimly. "Keep me informed."

Left alone, he turned back toward Eva. She was smiling now, her father's hand clasped in hers, their profiles mirroring each other in the pale morning light streaming through the windows. This was what mattered—that she was safe, reunited with her father, free from Billington's clutches.

But for how long?

The constable's warning echoed in his mind. Billington had spent years building his criminal empire. He'd have protection, influence, powerful friends willing to look the other way. Without an equally powerful counterweight, he might yet escape justice.

James' fingers curled into fists at his sides. The Pembroke name carried weight, but his family's fortunes had been severely damaged by Billington's machinations. Their shipping business was in tatters, their investments compromised. What they needed now was an alliance—a strategic marriage that would restore their social and financial standing.

Lady Catherine Darrington's family possessed precisely the kind of influence that could ensure Billington faced the full force of the law. Her father sat on the King's Privy Council; her uncle was Lord Chief Justice. With the Darringtons' support, no amount of bribery could save Billington from transportation—or the gallows.

James closed his eyes briefly, the weight of his decision pressing down upon him. To protect Eva, to ensure her father's decade-long quest for justice succeed, to prevent Billington from ever hurting another soul—he would need to marry Lady Catherine.

He looked again at Eva, her face alight with joy despite her pain, and felt his heart constrict. Sometimes, he thought bitterly, love meant making impossible choices.

ENOUGH

𝓔va shifted against the crisp hospital linens, wincing as the movement sent fresh pain shooting through her bandaged leg. The small bed offered little comfort, but compared to the dormitories of Middleford or the factory floor, it was luxurious beyond measure. Sunlight streamed through the narrow window, illuminating the variety of flowers that brightened the otherwise sterile room—lilies, roses, and violets arranged in delicate bouquets that James brought each day.

"These will brighten your spirits," he'd said yesterday, placing fresh daffodils on her bedside table. His fingers had lingered near hers, not quite touching. "The doctor says you're healing remarkably well."

Eva inhaled their sweet perfume now, letting the scent transport her beyond these walls. Her father had gone to speak with authorities about Billington's arrest, leaving her alone with her thoughts and the constant parade of nurses checking her bandages.

The door creaked open, and James entered, carrying yet another bouquet—wild bluebells this time, their delicate heads nodding with each step he took.

"You'll turn this room into a garden if you continue," Eva said, smiling despite the tightness in her chest. Something had changed in him since the fire. Behind his warm gaze lurked shadows she couldn't quite name.

"Then I shall have succeeded in my mission." He arranged the bluebells beside her bed, his movements precise, almost formal. "How are you feeling today?"

"Better. The doctor says I might walk short distances tomorrow."

"That's excellent news." His smile didn't quite reach his eyes.

Eva studied him—the tense set of his shoulders, the barely perceptible furrow between his brows. She'd seen that look before, on her Father's face when navigating treacherous waters, on Mrs Fisher's when calculating whether she could afford to keep Eva another month.

"James," she said softly, "what troubles you?"

He sank into the chair beside her bed, shoulders slumping. "Billington's arrest isn't as straightforward as we'd hoped. The constable warns he has influential friends."

"But surely, with all the evidence against him—"

"Evidence can disappear. Witnesses can be silenced." His voice hardened. "Money speaks volumes in the courts."

The room fell silent save for the distant sounds of the hospital corridor. Eva reached for his hand, her fingers brushing his. "Your family? Have they pressured you about this?"

James' jaw tightened. "They're concerned about our standing, yes. The shipping business has suffered greatly from Billington's sabotage."

"And Lady Catherine's family could help secure justice," Eva finished quietly.

His eyes met hers, startled. "How did you—"

"I've spent my life watching people, James. Learning what

they want, what they fear." She managed a smile that felt brittle on her lips. "It's how I survived."

James leaned forward, taking her hands in his with sudden intensity. "None of it changes what I feel for you, Eva. You must believe that."

"I do," she whispered.

"The things we've endured these past weeks ... they've only proven the value of what matters most." His thumb traced circles on her palm. "When I thought I might lose you in that fire—"

"But you didn't," Eva reminded him. "We're both here."

"Yes." His gaze dropped to their intertwined fingers. "Though the aftermath has been ... complicated. My uncle estimates the family has lost nearly a third of our assets through Billington's schemes. The docklands alone will require significant investment to restore."

The implication hung in the air between them, unspoken yet unmistakable. Eva fought against the tears threatening to well in her eyes, recalling the cruel judgment in Aunt Agatha's expression at their one brief meeting. A seamstress was no match for a noble family's legacy.

"Is it enough?" Eva asked finally, her voice barely audible.

James looked up, confusion crossing his features. "Is what enough?"

"This." She gestured between them. "What we feel. Is it strong enough to withstand everything that stands against it?"

Eva thought of the workhouse, of the countless nights she'd endured through faith and determination alone. She'd survived starvation, cruelty, and fire—yet this uncertainty seemed more terrifying than any of those trials.

"I've lost everything before," she continued when he didn't immediately answer. "My mother, my father—though miraculously, I have him back now. I survived with nothing but the clothes on my back and the memory of being loved." Her voice strengthened. "I could do it again if necessary."

James' grip tightened on her hands, his expression tormented. "Eva, I—"

The door swung open, revealing a nurse with a tray of medicines. "Time for your tonics, Miss Hartwell," she announced cheerfully, oblivious to the moment she'd interrupted.

James released Eva's hands and stood, his face composed once more into the polite mask of nobility. "I should let you rest," he said, his voice strained. "I'll return tomorrow."

As he left, Eva turned her face toward the window, allowing a single tear to trace its path down her cheek. Outside, London continued its relentless pace, indifferent to the battles being waged in hearts throughout the city.

LADY CATHERINE

James stared at his reflection in the carriage window, barely recognizing the man who gazed back. Dark circles shadowed his eyes, remnants of sleepless nights spent agonising over impossible choices. His chest felt hollow, like something vital had been carved out. Perhaps it had been—his heart remained in that hospital room with Eva.

The carriage slowed before the Darrington estate, a sprawling Georgian mansion nestled amid manicured gardens. Each revolution of the wheels brought him closer to his duty and further from his desire. The documents in his breast pocket —an agreement drafted by his solicitor regarding the proposed union between the Pembroke and Darrington families— weighed heavier than iron.

He'd rehearsed the words a dozen times. They tasted of ash.

The footman opened the carriage door with a polite bow. "Lord Pembroke. Lady Darrington is expecting you in the blue drawing room."

James nodded, straightening his shoulders. He'd face this like his father would have—with dignity and resolve, sacrificing personal happiness for the greater good. Eva deserved justice. The workers who'd suffered under Billington's cruel regime deserved justice. If securing that justice required him to honour his family's wishes, then so be it.

The butler announced him with practiced formality. James entered the drawing room, its elegant blue and gold décor befitting the wealth of the Darrington family. Lady Catherine stood by the window, her golden hair catching the afternoon light. She turned, her posture perfect, her expression unreadable.

"Lord Pembroke," she said, offering a slight curtsy. "How unexpected."

James bowed. "Lady Catherine. Thank you for receiving me without prior notice."

"Please, sit." She gestured to the sofa across from her chair. "Tea?"

"No, thank you." He remained standing, hands clasped behind his back. Better to proceed directly. Prolonging this would only make it more difficult. "I've come on a matter of some importance."

Something flickered across her face—resignation, perhaps. "I suspected as much. Your expression is quite grave."

James cleared his throat. "Lady Catherine, our families have long discussed the possibility of an alliance between us. Recent events have convinced me of the wisdom of such an arrangement."

Her eyebrow arched slightly. "Recent events? You mean the scandal with the fire at Billington's factory? The one where you nearly perished rescuing a seamstress?"

Heat crept up James' neck. "The situation is more complex than the gossip columns suggest. Billington is a criminal who's exploited countless innocent people. He kidnapped Miss Hartwell to manipulate me into surrendering my family's business interests."

"And now you need my family's influence to ensure he faces

THE CAPTAIN'S LOST DAUGHTER

justice," Lady Catherine finished, her tone matter-of-fact. "So you've come to propose marriage."

James blinked, surprised by her directness. "I—yes."

Lady Catherine rose from her chair and walked to a small writing desk in the corner. She opened a drawer and withdrew a folded document, which she handed to him.

"What's this?" James asked, unfolding the paper.

"Read it."

His eyes widened as he scanned the contents. It was a detailed legal statement describing illicit business dealings between Marcus Billington and several members of Parliament, complete with dates, figures, and specific violations of the law.

"How did you obtain this?" he asked, stunned.

"My father may appear to be merely a social butterfly, but he has comprehensive records of every business transaction he's ever witnessed or heard discussed. Billington approached him two years ago with a scheme involving workhouse contracts." A smile touched her lips. "Father declined, but kept notes. He's fastidious that way."

"This is ... extraordinary," James murmured, still reviewing the document. "With this evidence—"

"Billington will face the full force of the law, regardless of his connections," Lady Catherine finished. "My father has already spoken with the Lord Chancellor. The case will receive the highest scrutiny."

James stared at her, bewildered. "I don't understand. Why would you help me like this?"

"The seamstress—Miss Hartwell—she helped me choose fabrics." Lady Catherine's voice softened. "I've been measured and fitted by countless dressmakers since childhood. They all treat me the same way—as a noble body to be draped in finery, a walking exhibition of their craft, a walking purse."

She turned to face him. "But Miss Hartwell was different. She looked at me and saw a woman with preferences and feelings. She asked questions about what I enjoyed, what made me feel confident. It was a small thing, perhaps, but in that moment, I wasn't a bargaining chip in some alliance between families. I was simply Catherine."

James felt something tighten in his chest. "That is ... very much like her."

"I want you to marry her, Lord Pembroke." Lady Catherine's green eyes held his steadily. "My family's influence will ensure Billington faces justice, and I'll make it quite clear to society that I chose to end our potential engagement, not you. Your reputation will remain intact."

"But why would you do this?"

"Because I want what Miss Hartwell had the wisdom to offer me—the chance to be seen as a person, not a position." Her lips curved in a small smile. "And because I've seen the way you look at her. I would rather not spend my life with a man whose heart belongs elsewhere."

The door burst open before James could respond. Scarlett rushed in, her cheeks flushed.

"I knew it!" She flung her arms around Lady Catherine, who stiffened in surprise before awkwardly returning the embrace. "I heard everything from the corridor, and I just couldn't contain myself a moment longer. My carriage was just behind his."

"Lady Scarlett," Catherine murmured, flustered by the unexpected contact. "This is most irregular."

"Oh, forget propriety," Scarlett laughed, releasing her. "You've just saved my brother from a lifetime of misery and possibly rescued the most wonderful love story I've ever witnessed." She clasped Catherine's hands. "You must come to the wedding. And we shall be the greatest of friends."

James watched, dumbfounded, as his sister chattered excitedly about plans and possibilities. The weight that had pressed upon his chest for days lifted, replaced by a lightness he hadn't felt since watching Eva read poetry in the park, sunlight catching in her golden curls.

"Lady Catherine," he said finally, drawing both women's attention. "I don't know how to thank you."

She met his gaze evenly. "Be happy, Lord Pembroke. That will be thanks enough."

NEW BEGINNINGS

*E*va stood at the window of her bedroom above Thornton's shop, watching the morning light spill across London's rooftops. The city looked different somehow—cleaner, brighter, full of possibility. Her fingers traced the fading scars on her palms, battle wounds from the factory fire three months prior.

The bell downstairs chimed. Miss Adelaide's voice drifted up, greeting an early customer. Eva smiled, grateful for the routine that had resumed after weeks of chaos. The newspapers had been filled with accounts of Billington's trial, each day revealing new horrors about his business empire. Factory conditions, fraudulent documents, bribery of officials—the list seemed endless.

Eva turned from the window and smoothed her simple blue dress. Today marked her return to full duties at the shop after her recovery. She'd insisted, despite her father and James both suggesting she might rest longer.

"I've had quite enough of resting," she murmured to herself, pinning her hair neatly.

When she descended the stairs, she found not a customer waiting, but William, smartly dressed in a merchant's coat.

"Good morning, shipwreck survivor," he said with a grin that still held traces of the twelve-year-old boy she'd known on the SS Lydia.

"William!" Eva embraced him warmly. "I thought you'd returned to Liverpool."

"Only briefly. I've business in London now—good business." His eyes sparkled with excitement. "Billington's shipping contracts have been redistributed by the courts. With Lord Pembroke's recommendation, I've secured three of them."

Miss Adelaide appeared from the back room, carrying a bolt of emerald silk. "Mr Ansley brings excellent news, Eva. It seems the Billington verdict has created quite the stir."

"Life imprisonment," William confirmed. "And the judge made a rather poetic statement about justice finally reaching those who believed themselves beyond its grasp."

Eva felt a weight lift from her shoulders—one she hadn't fully acknowledged until this moment. "And the children from the factory?"

"Most have been placed with families through the church programs. Lord Pembroke's sister has been particularly tireless in that effort."

Eva smiled, thinking of Scarlett's passionate determination to ensure every child found proper care. "And Mary? The girl with the red hair?"

"Apprenticed to a milliner in Covent Garden," William replied. "She has quite the eye for design, according to the woman who took her in."

Eva's father entered the shop, the bell announcing his arrival. Captain Thomas Hartwell looked younger these days, the lines of worry gradually fading from his face. He carried a newspaper tucked under his arm.

"Have you told her?" he asked William eagerly.

"I was just getting to that part," William replied. "The Pembroke shipping offices are reopening today. The court has fully restored their ownership of the dock properties that Billington tried to seize."

Eva's heart quickened. "That's wonderful news."

"Indeed," her father agreed. "And there's more. Lord Pembroke has instituted new policies for all workers on his properties—fair wages, limited hours, proper safety measures." He unfolded the newspaper, pointing to an article. "They're calling it 'The Pembroke Reform.'"

Miss Adelaide squeezed Eva's hand. "He's been quite busy these past weeks, hasn't he?"

Eva nodded, thinking of James' brief visits, always polite, always proper. Since the fire, something had shifted between them—not cooling, exactly, but careful, as though both were afraid to disturb a delicate balance.

The bell chimed again. Eva turned, and there stood James himself, looking somewhat nervous despite his formal attire.

"Good morning," he said, his eyes finding Eva immediately.

"What a happy coincidence," William said, exchanging a knowing glance with Thomas. "The captain and I were just heading out to inspect the docks. Miss Adelaide, might you accompany us? I believe there was that matter of the imported lace you wanted to inquire about."

Miss Adelaide, who had made no such inquiry to Eva's knowledge, nodded enthusiastically. "Yes, indeed. Most urgent."

The three departed with suspicious haste, leaving Eva and James alone in the shop's front room. Sunlight streamed through the display window, catching on the fabric samples and creating patterns across the wooden floor.

"I've news," James said, stepping closer.

"So I've heard. The docks, the reforms—it's all wonderful, James."

He shook his head. "That's not why I'm here." He took a deep breath. "Eva, I've come to realise something these past months. When I nearly lost you in that fire, when I saw everything I owned potentially slipping away—I understood what truly matters."

He took her hands in his. Eva noticed he was trembling slightly.

"What matters is not the ships or the docks or the family name. What matters is you. Your courage, your spirit, your heart that sees people for who they truly are." He reached into his pocket and withdrew a small velvet box. "I love you, Evangeline Hartwell. I want to build a life with you—not the life my family expected, but something better, something real."

He opened the box, revealing a ring with a sapphire surrounded by tiny diamonds, like stars around the moon.

"Will you marry me?"

Eva looked from the ring to his face, seeing all the hope and love and future possibilities reflected there. Spring sunshine warmed her skin as she thought of their journey—from strangers to friends to something deeper than she'd ever imagined possible.

"Yes," she whispered, feeling tears of joy well in her eyes. "Yes, James, I will."

When he slipped the ring onto her finger, it fit perfectly—just as their hands fit together, just as their hearts had found their match across the divisions of class and circumstance.

FOREVER AFTER

The church bells of St Anne's chimed across London on a perfect July morning, their jubilant peals carrying over the harbour where ships rocked gently at their moorings. Inside the stone church, Eva stood in a small antechamber, watching sunlight filter through stained glass and transform ordinary dust motes into floating jewels.

"Almost ready, my dear?" Miss Adelaide fussed with the fall of Eva's wedding gown—a creation they had designed together during countless evenings at the shop.

Eva touched the delicate lace at her sleeves, marvelling at how her trembling fingers could have crafted something so fine. The ivory silk shimmered as she turned, cascading from a fitted bodice to a graceful skirt adorned with embroidered flowers that seemed to bloom with each movement.

"You look absolutely radiant," Scarlett declared, stepping back to admire her handiwork after adjusting Eva's veil. "James will be utterly speechless."

Eva smiled at her soon-to-be sister-in-law. "I can only hope so."

The women laughed, and Eva felt a surge of gratitude for

THE CAPTAIN'S LOST DAUGHTER

how completely Scarlett had welcomed her into the family, championing their match even when others had initially whispered about its impropriety.

A gentle knock interrupted their preparations. "May I come in?" Captain Thomas Hartwell's voice carried through the door.

"Of course, Father." Eva smoothed her skirts one final time as he entered.

Her father halted in the doorway, his weathered hand rising to his heart. For a moment, he couldn't speak, his eyes shining with unshed tears.

"Oh, my little girl." His voice caught. "You look just like your mother on our wedding day."

Eva crossed to him, careful of her dress. "I was hoping you'd say that."

"She would have been so proud of you, Eva." He offered his arm. "I believe they're ready for us. Shall we?"

Eva took his arm, feeling the solid strength that had carried her through their reunion and healing. "Ready, Captain."

The church doors opened to reveal a sanctuary transformed. Wildflowers and sea lavender adorned every pew, their subtle fragrance mingling with beeswax candles. Sunlight streamed through the windows, casting golden pathways across the stone floor.

But it was the faces that truly took Eva's breath away.

The church overflowed with people whose lives had become intertwined with hers. Near the front sat Charlie, now a young man apprenticed to a printer, alongside Betsy and Samuel from the workhouse, scrubbed clean and wearing new clothes, their faces alight with excitement. Behind them, Mary from the factory beamed, her red hair elegantly arranged beneath a milliner's creation of her own design.

Mrs Fisher from the fishing village dabbed at her eyes with a handkerchief, seated beside Mrs Beasley, whose stern workhouse demeanour had softened since finding employment at the newly established Hartwell Foundation. Even Barrett, Billington's former assistant, sat in a back pew, his posture reflecting both discomfort and gratitude for the second chance James had offered him.

Eva spotted Lucy, the match girl who had first shown her where to sleep in London, now dressed as a proper lady's maid in Miss Adelaide's employ. Beside her sat Mr Finch from the Whistling Sailor tavern, looking rather uncomfortable in his Sunday best.

Lady Catherine, who had been so integral in securing justice for Mr Billington, sat beside Scarlett.

And then, standing at the altar, was James. His eyes locked with hers the moment she appeared, and everything else seemed to fade away. William stood beside him as best man, a newfound friend and now his most trusted advisor, both in business and in matters of the heart.

Eva and her father began their slow procession down the aisle as the organ swelled. With each step, Eva felt the weight of her journey—the terror of the shipwreck, the despair of the workhouse, the struggle on London's streets, and finally, the joy of finding love and family once more.

"Who gives this woman to be married?" the vicar asked when they reached the altar.

Her father cleared his throat. "I do, her father." His voice carried clearly through the church, filled with pride and joy, before he placed Eva's hand in James' and stepped back.

James squeezed her fingers gently, his eyes never leaving hers. "You are magnificent," he whispered, too softly for anyone but Eva to hear.

The ceremony proceeded with ancient words and timeless promises. When they exchanged rings, Eva noticed James' hands were as unsteady as her own, and the shared vulnerability made her love him all the more.

"I, James, take thee, Evangeline, to be my wedded wife, to

have and to hold from this day forward, for better for worse, for richer, for poorer, in sickness and in health, to love and to cherish, till death us do part, according to God's holy ordinance; and thereto I plight thee my troth."

Each word resonated through Eva's heart as she repeated her own vows, thinking of how completely they had already lived these promises—through fire and danger, through loss and recovery.

"I now pronounce you man and wife," the vicar declared. "You may kiss your bride."

James cupped Eva's face with tender reverence before leaning forward to seal their union with a kiss that promised a lifetime of devotion.

The congregation erupted in cheers and applause as they turned to face their assembled loved ones. Eva caught sight of Charlie leading the younger children in an enthusiastic display that bordered on impropriety for church, but the vicar merely smiled indulgently.

Hand in hand, they proceeded back down the aisle and out into the London sunshine, where the real celebration would begin.

THE HARTWELL FOUNDATION

The Pembroke country estate had been transformed for the occasion. The sprawling gardens now featured white tents adorned with wildflowers and sea lavender, tables laden with food, and a wooden dance floor constructed especially for the celebration.

But the true centrepiece stood on the estate's eastern lawn: a new building of red brick and large windows, its doors thrown open to welcome guests for its inaugural day.

"The Hartwell Foundation," Eva read the engraved stone above the entrance, her heart swelling with pride.

"Do you like it?" James asked, his arm around her waist. "Scarlett insisted on having it ready in time for today."

"It's perfect," Eva whispered, watching as children from the workhouses and factories explored the bright classrooms filled with books, art supplies, and educational materials. "A place where they can learn, grow, and discover their own strength."

Eva gazed at the classrooms, her mind's eye filling them with the multitude of happy children that will pass through them. As she stood musing, her mind drifted to all those she'd met on her journey—Charlie, Samuel, the children from Billington's factory, and countless others still struggling on London's streets. This foundation would reach them all, offering education when society had abandoned them.

The school would teach not just letters and numbers, but practical skills too. With William's merchant connections and James's shipping enterprise, pathways awaited these children that Eva could only have dreamed of in the workhouse. Apprenticeships, positions, real chances for dignified lives.

Her father approached, accompanying an elderly gentleman Eva didn't recognise. "Eva, James—allow me to introduce Mr Bence, the new headmaster. He's spent thirty years teaching children of all backgrounds in Edinburgh."

"Mrs Pembroke," Mr Bence bowed slightly. "Lord Pembroke has told me of your vision for this place. I assure you, every child who passes through these doors will receive not only an education but the care and respect they deserve."

"Thank you, Mr Bence." Eva smiled, noticing how the man's kind eyes crinkled at the corners. "I hope you'll let me visit often. Perhaps I might even teach a sewing class occasionally."

"We would be honoured, ma'am," he replied. "And might I say, your story has inspired many of us to see these children differently—not as burdens to be managed, but as treasures waiting to be discovered."

As Mr Bence moved away to greet new arrivals, William approached with two glasses of champagne.

"A toast to the bride and groom," he declared, handing them each a glass. "And to new beginnings."

"To new beginnings," they echoed, clinking their glasses together.

The afternoon unfolded in a tapestry of joy. Children raced across the lawns while adults gathered in conversational clusters. The social barriers that might once have separated them—workhouse orphan from factory worker, dock worker from merchant, lady from seamstress—seemed to dissolve in the shared celebration.

Eva found herself constantly surrounded by well-wishers, each with a story to tell or gratitude to express. Little Mary shyly presented her with a handkerchief she had embroidered herself. Charlie, now tall and gangly, showed her the apprentice certificate he'd earned at the printing house where James had placed him.

"I can read anything now," he told her proudly. "Even the hardest words."

"I never doubted you for a moment," Eva replied, remembering the determined boy who had traced letters in workhouse dust.

As twilight approached, lanterns were lit throughout the garden, creating pools of golden light. Musicians struck up a lively tune, and James appeared at Eva's side.

"May I have this dance, Mrs Pembroke?" he asked with a formal bow that was belied by the mischievous twinkle in his eyes.

"You may indeed, Lord Pembroke," she replied, allowing him to lead her to the centre of the floor.

They moved together in perfect harmony as other couples joined them—William with Scarlett, her father with Miss Adelaide, and even some of the older children attempting their first formal dance steps with varying degrees of success.

"Are you happy, my love?" James asked as he guided her through a turn.

Eva looked up at her husband's face, so dear and familiar now. "Completely. Are you?"

"More than I ever imagined possible." He drew her closer than was strictly proper for a public dance. "Though I must warn you, Aunt Agatha is still somewhat scandalised that I married a seamstress."

Eva laughed. "And yet here she is, teaching Mary how to properly hold a teacup. I believe we're winning her over."

As the dance ended, her father approached and claimed Eva for the next set, his movements still carrying the disciplined grace of his naval days.

"Your mother would be so proud," he said as they circled the floor. "Not just of your marriage, but of what you've built here—this foundation, these connections. You've taken all the hardship life dealt you and transformed it into something beautiful."

"We both have, Father." Eva squeezed his hand. "Remember when you told me I was fiercer than any storm? I think perhaps I inherited that from you."

The evening continued with feasting, dancing, and laughter. As darkness fell completely, William called for everyone's attention, raising his glass for a toast.

"To James and Evangeline," he began, his voice carrying across the gathering. "Two souls who found each other across an ocean of circumstances that might have kept them apart."

He turned to face them directly. "And especially to Eva, whom I first met as a golden-haired child on the deck of the SS Lydia, watching the stars with wonder. Your courage has never wavered, from that terrible night of the storm to today. You've shown us all what it means to face life's worst moments and still believe in its best possibilities."

"To James and Eva," the crowd echoed, raising their glasses.

Later, as the celebration continued around them, James led Eva to a quiet corner of the garden where a stone bench overlooked the moonlit grounds. In the distance, they could see the Hartwell Foundation building, its windows glowing warmly in the night.

"What are you thinking?" James asked, his arm around her shoulders.

Eva leaned against him, treasuring the solid warmth of his

presence. "I'm thinking about journeys. How the worst storm can sometimes carry you exactly where you need to be."

James pressed a kiss to her temple. "Even if it takes ten years and countless trials to arrive?"

"Especially then." Eva turned to face him fully. "Because then you know exactly how precious the destination is."

Their kiss was gentle and unhurried, a promise of all the days stretching before them. Around them, the celebration continued—children laughing, music playing, lives rebuilding after darkness. And above them, stars wheeled in their ancient patterns, lighting paths for travellers both at sea and at home.

THE FIRST CHAPTER OF 'THE ORPHAN'S LETTERS TO PROVIDENCE'

The sun rose gently over the Yorkshire landscape, painting the modest parsonage in hues of amber and gold. Light filtered through the thin curtains of Alice's small bedroom, casting dancing patterns across her eyelids. She stirred beneath her blanket, the familiar sounds of morning birds coaxing her from slumber.

Alice opened her eyes, blinking away the remnants of sleep. Eleven years old and already accustomed to the rhythm of early mornings, she took a moment to appreciate the quiet stillness before the day began in earnest. The wooden floorboards creaked beneath her as she stretched her limbs, feeling the pleasant ache of growing bones.

With practiced movements, Alice slipped from her bed and reached for the simple brown dress hanging on the hook by her wardrobe. The fabric was worn at the elbows, but clean and carefully mended. She dressed quickly, fingers deftly doing up the buttons before tying her apron around her waist. The apron had once been white but now bore the faint shadows of countless meals prepared and surfaces cleaned.

In the small kitchen, Alice moved with quiet efficiency. She stoked the dying embers in the stove, adding kindling until flames licked upward. The porridge oats went into the pot with water and a pinch of salt—no milk today, as they'd run out yesterday. As she stirred, Alice softly sang "Rock of Ages," her father's favourite hymn, her young voice clear in the morning quiet.

"That's a fine tune to greet the day with."

Alice turned to find her father standing in the doorway. Reverend Thomas Wells' salt-and-pepper hair stood slightly ruffled, as if he'd run his fingers through it while pondering some theological question before coming downstairs.

"Good morning, Father." Alice smiled, continuing to stir the thickening porridge.

"You've become quite the little housekeeper." He crossed the room and placed a gentle hand on her shoulder. "Your mother would be proud of how you've grown."

Alice's heart warmed at the rare mention of her mother. She ladled the porridge into two bowls and placed them on the small wooden table where they took their meals.

"Mrs Pemberton's youngest has the croup," Reverend Wells said between spoonfuls. "I thought we might visit them this morning, bring some of that honey from Mr Thompson."

"The Pembertons live near the mill, don't they?" Alice asked, her interest piqued. "Will we see the workers changing shifts?"

Her father nodded. "Indeed. Though I worry for those children. Some a bit younger than you, working such long hours in dangerous conditions."

"Is that why you spoke about the Good Samaritan in Sunday's sermon? Because of the mill children?"

Reverend Wells looked at his daughter with surprised appreciation. "You've a keen mind, Alice. Yes, I believe our Christian duty extends to all neighbours, especially those most vulnerable. Mr Pullman didn't seem to appreciate the message, however."

"But it was from Scripture," Alice reasoned, her brow furrowed in thought. "Surely he cannot argue with the Lord's teachings?"

"Men find ways to interpret God's word to suit their purposes." Her father sighed. "But that doesn't make it right."

**Click here to read the rest of
'The Orphan's Letters to Providence'**

When Words Become Prayers. When Love Becomes Strength.

In the windswept Yorkshire countryside, Alice Wells's world

shatters when tragedy strikes her beloved parents. Orphaned and thrust into a hostile household, she clings to his dying words: "Write to Providence, dear heart."

Stripped of everything but her faith, Alice begins pouring her heart into secret letters addressed to God himself. These hidden journals become her lifeline as she endures years of servitude and growing danger in the home of those who would see her broken.

When William Thornton arrives as tutor to the son of the head of the household, Alice discovers an unexpected ally. Their stolen moments of conversation kindle into something deeper — a love that transcends the rigid boundaries of society. But in a world where power crushes the innocent, their forbidden connection may prove more dangerous than either imagined.

As Alice witnesses injustice that echoes her father's own struggles, she faces impossible choices. Will she find the courage to stand against those who destroyed her family? Can William's love give her strength when the final reckoning comes? And will their faith prove stronger than the forces that threaten to tear them apart?

Can Alice's letters to Providence sustain her through the trials ahead? Will love prove stronger than the forces seeking to destroy her? And in her darkest hour, can faith truly illuminate the path to redemption?

'The Orphan's Letters to Providence'

OUR GIFT TO YOU

AS A WAY TO SAY THANK YOU WE WOULD LOVE TO SEND YOU THIS BEAUTIFUL STORY FREE OF CHARGE.

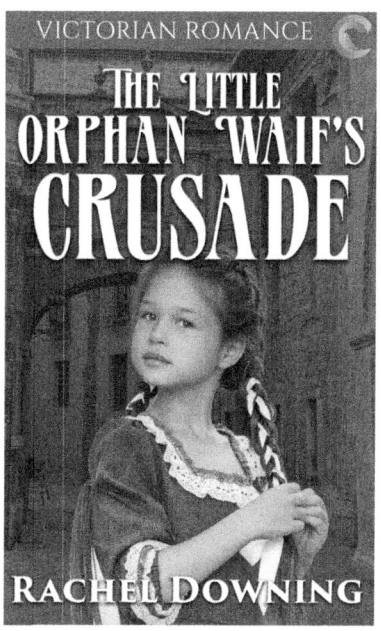

Click here for your FREE COPY of
"The Little Orphan Waif's Crusade'
CornerstoneTales.com/sign-up

In the wake of her father's passing, seven-year-old Matilda is determined to heal her sister Effie's shattered spirit.

Desperate to restore joy to Effie's life, Matilda embarks on a daring quest, aided by the gentle-hearted postman, Philip. Together, they weave a plan to ignite the flame of love in Effie's heart once more.

At Cornerstone Tales we publish books you can trust. Great tales without sex or swearing, but with all of the mystery and romance you expect from a great story.

Be the first to know when we release new books, take part in our fun competitions, and get surprise free books in your inbox by signing up to our free VIP Reader list.

As a thank you you'll receive a copy of 'The Little Orphan Waif's Crusade' straight away, alongside other gifts.

Click here to sign up for our mailing list, and receive your FREE stories.

CornerstoneTales.com/sign-up

LOVE VICTORIAN ROMANCE?

Other Rachel Downing Books

The Orphan's Letters to Providence

In the windswept Yorkshire countryside, Alice Wells's world shatters when tragedy strikes her beloved parents. Orphaned and thrust into a hostile household, she clings to his dying words: "Write to Providence, dear heart."

Get 'The Orphan's Letters to Providence' Here!

The Forsaken Lacemaker of Hampstead

In the shadow of Victorian London, Mabel Fairchild's life is shattered by false accusations and devastating loss. With two younger siblings dependent on her care, she makes an impossible promise: to keep her family together despite the world's cruel intentions.

Get 'The Forsaken Lacemaker of Hampstead' Here!

The Workhouse Orphan's Redemption

In the brutal world of Victorian London, Emma Redbrook's life begins in tragedy. Orphaned and trapped in Grimshaw's Workhouse, she endures cruelty that would break most spirits. But Emma's unwavering faith becomes her beacon of hope — and her strength.

Get 'The Workhouse Orphan's Redemption' Here!

The Orphan's Christmas Hymn

Seven-year-old Clara Winters' world shatters when tragedy strikes days before Christmas. Sent to St. Mary's Church Orphanage, she finds her only solace in the hymns that once filled her happy home. When her angelic voice catches the attention of the kind-hearted Reverend Thornton and his musically gifted son Edward, Clara dares to dream of a brighter future.

Get 'The Orphan's Christmas Hymn' Here!

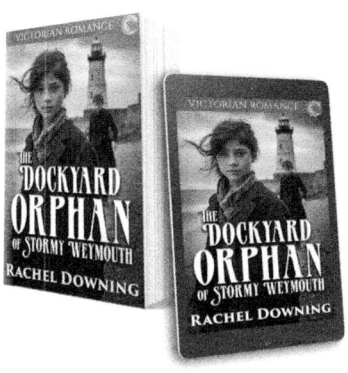

The Dockyard Orphan of Stormy Weymouth

Sarah Campbell's world crumbles when a tragic accident claims her parents' lives. She finds solace in the lighthouse's beam that guides ships to safety. But it's a young fisherman wrestling with his own loss, who truly captures her heart.

Get 'The Dockyard Orphan of Stormy Weymouth' Here!

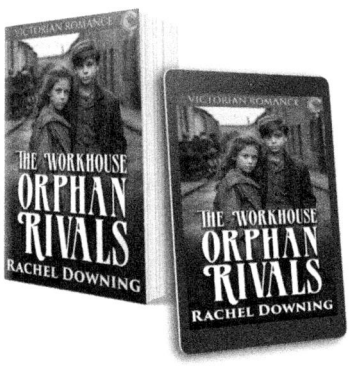

The Workhouse Orphan Rivals

Childhood sweethearts torn apart. A promise broken. A love that refuses to die.

Get 'The Workhouse Orphan Rivals' Here!

The Orphan Prodigy's Stolen Tale

When ten-year-old Isabella Farmerson's world shatters with the tragic loss of her parents, she's thrust into a life of hardship and uncertainty.

Get 'The Orphan Prodigy's Stolen Tale' Here!

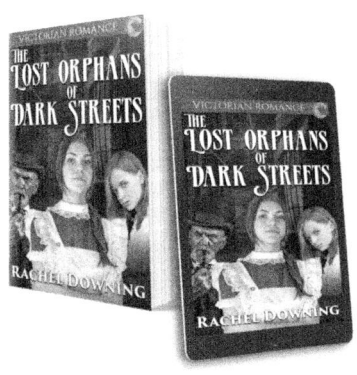

The Lost Orphans of Dark Streets

Follow the stories of Elizabeth and Molly as they negotiate the dangerous slums and find their place in the world.

Get 'The Lost Orphans of Dark Streets' Here!

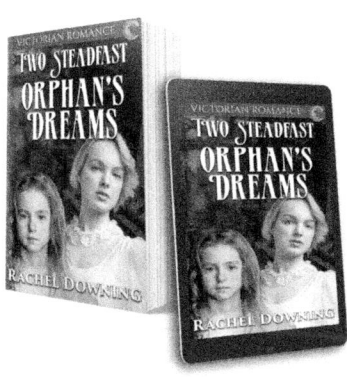

Two Steadfast Orphan's Dreams

Follow the stories of Isabella and Ada as they overcome all odds and find love.

Get 'Two Steadfast Orphan's Dreams' Here!

And from our other Victorian Romance Author Dorothy Wellings…

The Moral Maid's Unjust Trial

Matilda must fend for herself when her father is wrongfully accused for a crime he didn't commit.

Get 'The Moral Maid's Unjust Trial' Here!

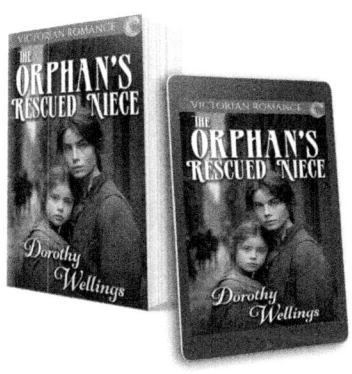

The Orphan's Rescued Niece

As Beatrice grows from a wide-eyed child into a resilient young woman, she finds herself caught between her love for her troubled brother and her desire for a life free from poverty and fear.

Get 'The Orphan's Rescued Niece' Here!

The Lost Orphan of the Parish

Annabelle's world shatters when illness claims her beloved parents. Left alone at ten years old with no inheritance, she's sent to the harsh Thornfield Orphanage with nothing but her father's worn Bible and the memories of his gentle teachings.

Get 'The Lost Orphan of the Parish' Here!

The Orphan Angel's Grace

Grace Hartwell's world is illuminated by her father's love and the warm glow of London's gas lamps he tends each night. Living humbly but happily above a Whitechapel bakery, ten-year-old Grace treasures her father's stories of her saintly mother and learns the healing arts from her mother's cherished prayer book.

Get 'The Orphan Angel's Grace' Here!

If you enjoyed this story, sign up to our mailing list to be the first to hear about our new releases and any sales and deals we have.

We also want to offer you a Victorian Romance novella - 'The Little Orphan Waif's Crusade' - absolutely free!

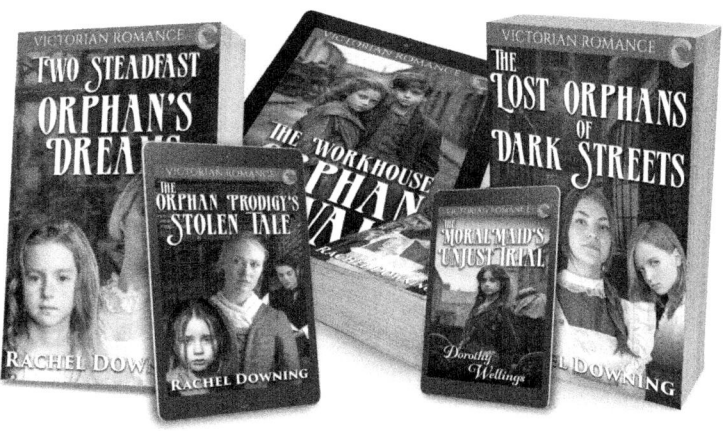

Click here to sign up for our mailing list, and receive your FREE stories.

CornerstoneTales.com/sign-up

Printed in Dunstable, United Kingdom